TWISTER

JULIETTE FORREST

In memory of Pete

Scholastic Children's Books
An imprint of Scholastic Ltd
Euston House, 24 Eversholt Street, London, NW1 1DB, UK
Registered office: Westfield Road, Southam, Warwickshire, CV47 0RA
SCHOLASTIC and associated logos are trademarks and/or
registered trademarks of Scholastic Inc.

First published in the UK by Scholastic Ltd, 2018

Text copyright © Juliette Forrest, 2018
Illustrations copyright © Alexis Snell, 2018

The right of Juliette Forrest and Alexis Snell to be identified as the author and
illustrator of this work has been asserted by them.

ISBN 978 1407 18511 8

A CIP catalogue record for this book
is available from the British Library.

Printed by CPI Group (UK) Ltd, Croydon, CR0 4YY
Papers used by Scholastic Children's Books are made
from wood grown in sustainable forests.

1 3 5 7 9 10 8 6 4 2

This is a work of fiction. Names, characters, places, incidents
and dialogues are products of the author's imagination or are used
fictitiously. Any resemblance to actual people, living or dead,
events or locales is entirely coincidental.

www.scholastic.co.uk

When I appeared the sky glowed green and lightning made the windows look all cracked. Aunt Honey swore it was the worst storm in living memory. Ma said she worked out the time between each of her contractions by counting the roof tiles that flew past the window. And when she cussed with the pain, the wind carried her colourful words far away to another land.

Pa had paced up and down and up and down and up and down in the hallway. Ma screamed and the wind howled and the thunder thundered. And when the tips of the trees touched the ground, I wailed.

Pa rushed in to kiss Ma. He told me he grinned as wide as Eagle Creek when he held me. I wriggled around in his arms so much he called me Twister. It was a twister that had blown all the colour out of his hair.

I think I must have done something to scare him bad too. We ain't seen him in six months and three days and four hours.

Aunt Honey told me Pa disappearing plain broke Ma's heart. I guess if your heart was in pieces you'd feel poorly too.

Pa said Ma had the prettiest smile in Culleroy. Before he left she'd sing more than the birds. Now she was as quiet as her shadow. I always knew when Pa was in her thoughts though. She'd be here in the room with me, but she'd also be somewhere else too. Aunt Honey said it ain't possible for a person to be in two different places at the same time. But I think she was wrong 'bout that.

One time, when I was trying to sneak up on my

dog, Point, without waking him up, I heard Ma crying. I peeked through the crack in the door. Aunt Honey was telling Ma that there was nothing she could have done or said to drive Pa away 'cause he loved us more than anything else in the world. I guess Ma was blaming herself for his disappearance too.

I'm the spit of Pa. Except, my hair wasn't white. It was raspberry blonde. I had his blue, bluer-than-blue eyes though. But he don't have a gap between his front teeth to whistle through. I got that from Ma.

I learned to walk real fast. When I could run, Ma and Aunt Honey and Pa and Point chased me round and round and round the farm. I'd shriek with laughter. I made the chickens fly and the horses fly. I even made the pigs fly. If Pa catched me, he'd throw me into the air so I could touch heaven. Sometimes, I'd be so high up, I thought my head might clunk off the sun.

Ma decided not to send me to the school in Culleroy. She knew I'd the attention span of a buzzy-fly, so she took me outside to learn 'bout colours and shapes and plants and animals. And when she taught me spelling, we'd read out stories under the apple trees. Pa would sometimes stop by to see what we were giggling at. Sums

4

weren't quite so much fun though. Watching the black rooster on the barn roof twirling in the wind and Pa working in the fields and the clouds playing tag with each other across the sky happened to be way more interesting.

Clouds were great. I seen faces in them. And sometimes they'd turn into mermaids or dragons or skulls or swans. I loved how clouds were all sensitive. They'd change colour when they were sad and then they'd cry. I'd like me and Point to spend the day on one. And when we got tired from all that bouncing around, we'd sit and watch the land beneath us float by.

Ma don't teach me spelling or numbers no more. Not since Pa vanished. One morning soon afterwards, when she was in bed and Aunt Honey had left to sow the seeds, Point and me snuck out to see if we could find him. Point ran straight over to a bush and snuffled at it. But he found a fat old wood pigeon instead of Pa. Then I angered the ants with a stick. And catched butterflies with my hands. I also discovered skinks under rocks. They had three white lines on their backs and moved as quick as the wind. And some.

Point took me to where the rabbits lived. They'd dug lots of holes and left small, round dottles all over the grass. They sure did poop a lot.

The sun shone fierce, so we headed for the stream. Its brown water sang over green furry stones. Point showed me how to cool off by rolling in the mud. That made me laugh, but then I remembered 'bout Pa. We rushed back to see if he had come home. Ma and Aunt Honey were waiting for us in the kitchen. Ma's eyes were red and Aunt Honey frowned at me. She said never to go wandering off on my own again. Then she told Ma the whole of Culleroy would think I was being raised by mudskippers. She warned her that the time had come to let me go.

Thing is, she wasn't holding on to me in the first place.

Ma closed the doors in the house real loud and her sighs were so big they spun the black rooster on the barn round and round and round.

When the first white strawberries peeped out from underneath their scratchy leaves, Aunt Honey took me to the school in Culleroy. It smelled of wood and old paper and roses and chalk dust and sweetie breath and scuffed boots.

Aunt Honey winked at me before she left. Just as I thought it'd be a good idea to leave too, Miss Ida asked me to introduce myself to the class.

The girls were all prissy and the boys scowled. When I told them my name was Twister, they sniggered. My face changed its colour.

Miss Ida shushed them and asked me to speak 'bout myself. I wanted to say I was crazy 'bout going on adventures with Point and hunting for snickerbugs with Pa and watching butter slide off the hot pancakes I'd make with Ma. Boy, did I love that. But I seen them faces in front of me and mumbled I liked fishing instead. And shooglepopple candy. Everybody liked shooglepopple candy. Even prissy girls and scowling boys liked shooglepopple candy.

Miss Ida pointed to a girl who had a pink bow in her hair. "There's a seat next to Cherry Bonnwell."

"That ain't her chair. It's Lula's," muttered Cherry.

Miss Ida tutted. "You know fine well Lula's in a much better place. God rest her soul."

"Wish I was in a better place," said a boy who was slumped over his desk.

"Sit up properly, Clem Hussable. What have I told you about speaking out of turn? Extra homework for the rest of the week."

I stared at the empty seat.

"Go on, Twister. Sit yourself down," said Miss Ida.

Cherry gave me a look, as if I'd a catchy-disease, and moved her chair away.

"Where's Lula gone?" I whispered.

"You been locked away in a barn or something? She's gone to heaven, you loon. There was a fire in Holler Woods that killed her and her ma," hissed Cherry.

My mouth fallen open.

"Twister," said Miss Ida. "We don't talk in class unless we're invited to do so."

I gulped. I was sitting in a dead girl's seat. How had I not known 'bout a fire? Ma and Aunt Honey hadn't said nothing 'bout it. I guess I ain't been in the woods for a while. Not since Pa had left.

When Miss Ida started talking, I stopped wondering if the dead girl might haunt me for taking her chair. I even forgot to watch the clouds slide across the sky. Miss Ida told us stories 'bout the people who lived all over the world. There were men made of china and upside-down girls who followed the stars and boys who slept in houses made from ice.

Miss Ida had a globe on her desk. It reminded me of a pink and yellow and blue and green and purple gobstopper. I ain't licked it yet, but I betcha the sea tastes of blueberry. I hadn't realized the globe was so enormous. It sure was going to make finding Pa a whole lot harder

9

now. The sooner I brought him home, the faster Ma would get better. And then we'd all be happy again.

Miss Ida spoke to us 'bout new things every day. I'd be so amazed, she'd have to close my mouth with her hand.

I told anybody who'd listen what I'd learned. I whispered to Point there were cats in Africa so huge they'd chase *him*. He thumped his tail in the dust. The orange fire-breathing mountains astonished Aunt Honey so much, she burned the toast. I gathered together the spring peeper frogs and explained they used to be tadpoles. They weren't too happy 'bout that. It made them gulp. Ma sat up in bed when she heard me counting out the crows on the barn roof. But I didn't say nothing to the drunk man lying on the grass. Cherry Bonnwell told me he was the dead girl's pa, Turrety Knocks. He wouldn't care that you could find a pot of gold at the end of a rainbow. All he'd want was his wife and daughter back. I crouched down and fished my sandwich out of my bag. I left it next to him. I knew what it was like to miss someone you loved. But the difference was, I still had hope I'd see Pa again.

Clem Hussable don't care for me much. He said my brain was the size of a crumb. Clem sat at the back of the class. He had dirty hair and scabs and fallen-down socks. There was always something yucky coming out of his nose. And his mouth.

"Where's your pa?" he said.

"That ain't none of your business," I replied.

"He ran off 'cause he couldn't stand the sight of you. Nobody can. You don't have any friends," Clem said.

"You talk a load of old horse poop," I hurled back at him, though my guts did clench some. I guess the only real friend I had was Point. Unlike the girls in class, he was always pleased to see me. "For your information," I continued on. "Pa's on the other side of the world hunting for treasure."

That shut Clem up. But his spider-brown eyes followed me around. They were deep-set as if someone had pushed them hard into his skull. Maybe they had. Clem's pa, Hack Hussable, had two homes: one in Culleroy and one in Gravelswitch Jail.

Clem was smart 'cause he'd made friends with the stupidest boys. They thought he was hee-hoo funny. If someone cried at break time, you could bet your life Clem was behind it. Hair-pulling and head-slapping and arm-twisting and stomach-punching and wrist-burning and stick-poking and money-stealing. He done it all. And there was no use in telling Miss Ida 'bout it neither. Parker Harp did and look what happened to him. His leg got broken in two places. He told everyone he'd tripped down by Raging River but Dunk Torn said he'd seen Clem push Parker out of a tree.

Miss Ida had a ruler. She used it to whack you over the knuckles with if you weren't paying attention or you didn't understand something she'd already explained to you. I always had a red hand. When Miss Ida was talking 'bout sums or spelling, my mind would drift and I'd wonder where Pa was. The only time I'd listen was when she was reading a story or letting us make stuff in class.

I won a prize for building a boat that didn't go belly-up in the bucket. I constructed it out of two rusty cans and string and paper and a twig. Miss Ida said it was a remarkable feat of engineering.

I'd never won a prize before. The class clapped when Miss Ida handed me a yellow kite but only 'cause they were told to. Cherry pulled faces at me. I stopped smiling and examined the kite. It had a long tail made of different coloured bows. Rainbow bows. Point would go loopy-loo when he seen it flying. When I got back to my seat, someone had put a drawing pin on it. I flicked it off and glared at Cherry. She narrowed her eyes at me. If looks could kill, I'd be dead for sure.

After school, they took me by surprise. Clem and the boys had stopped breathing behind the grey crooked stones in the churchyard. When they jumped out, they whole scared me to death.

Clem stamped on my boat. The others used sticks to change the colour of my skin.

"Your pa's dead," said Clem.

"No he ain't!" I spat.

"White Eye got him 'cause he started that fire in Holler Woods."

"Everyone knows White Eye don't exist. You're stupider than I thought if you still believe those stories 'bout him," I said. "Besides, the only bad man in Culleroy is your pa!"

Clem grabbed my kite and snapped its frame. I kept my face still as walls. I would not give him the satisfaction of tears – not even when he ripped off its tail.

Every day after that Clem made sure I lost something: a button, an apple, a clump of hair, a tooth. And just when I thought he couldn't take nothing else from me, Clem whispered he'd cut out my tongue.

I stopped telling everyone what I learned. And I stopped winning stupid prizes too.

Miss Ida kept me behind after class. She always wore the same colour of blue that was on the back of a lady duck's wing. She smelled of that fancy talc in the pharmacy which stank of roses. But I don't know how 'cause there weren't any in it. And I should know; I took the lid off to rummage around inside.

Miss Ida's hair was tied up in a bun and the colour of autumn leaves. At the end of the day it looked like she'd been out in a storm 'cause her hair had mostly fallen down around her face.

Her eyes were as grey as rocks. I ain't seen the ones on the back of her head yet but she kept on telling us she had them. When she was writing on the board, she'd know if Cherry was chewing her nails or Bing Hardy was picking his nose.

Miss Ida cleared her throat. "Twister," she said. "What's wrong?"

"Nothing."

She brushed some chalk dust off her skirt.

"You never raise your hand in class any more," she said. "And your grades are slipping. Is it because of your pa? Has there been any news about him?" Miss Ida's eyes gleamed, eager to hear my answer. "We pray for you all in church, but you'd know that if your family found the time to come along."

I fixed my eyes on a picture of a cabin in the woods on the wall. I wished I was there instead.

Miss Ida straightened up and shifted in her seat. "I know things haven't been easy, but I can't help you until you tell me what the matter is."

"There ain't nothing to tell," I said with a shrug.

"I see," she said, removing her glasses to rub her eyes. The way people done when they were too tired to think in a straight line. She put her glasses back on and sighed. "Twister, if you fall any further behind in class, I'll have to let your ma know and I'll give you extra homework every night. Do you understand?"

"Yes, Miss Ida."

"Off you go then," she said.

I walked towards the door.

"Twister?"

"Miss Ida?"

"Could you bring some snickerbugs in on Monday? I'm doing a lesson on nocturnal creatures and it would be much appreciated."

"Uh-huh."

"It's *'Yes, Miss Ida'*."

"Yes, Miss Ida."

She began to tidy her desk, which was a sign I was free to leave. I felt kinda sad I couldn't tell her 'bout Clem and all. But I valued the use of my legs way more.

Outside the sun blazed and the wind played in the trees. Trees were the best. Not just 'cause you could climb them but 'cause they talked to each other. They waved their branches and shook their leaves as if they were laughing. Or they'd just heard some oh-my-golly-gosh gossip. And they were real clever too. Aunt Honey said their roots grew deeper and stronger in a storm.

I decided to go to Raging River. Nothing cooled you off faster than sticking your feet in the water. When I got there, I seen Clem and the boys. Their heads snapped up. And they approached me like a pack of dogs, eager for a kill.

Clem stepped forward. Mud was smeared across his face. "Did you squeal to Miss Ida, Twister?"

"Nope." I shook my head.

"I think that no-good tongue of yours is lying again," he said. "Your pa ain't searching for treasure. White Eye's stolen his soul and buried him six foot under 'cause he's guilty as sin. Your pa murdered Lula and her ma. Everyone knows he did."

His words stung more than wasps.

"If White Eye was real, he'd have come for your pa a long time ago," I spat.

Clem's face turned raspberry. The boys crept closer with their fists balled-up. There were five of them and one of me. The air was thick and heavy. Quick as a flash, a cold knife scratched at my throat.

"Old oily Ollie oils old oily autos," said Clem.

The boys glanced at each other.

"That's a tongue-twister . . . and here's Twister's tongue."

One of Clem's hands gripped the back of my neck. His nails dug into my skin. His other hand forced its way into my mouth. I closed my eyes and bit down as hard as I could.

I tasted grit and salt and metal.

Clem made the same noise as a baby rabbit catched in a dog's jaws and let me go.

Raging River blurred and the grass blurred and the trees blurred. When I finally stopped running, I'd no breath left. I found myself by a shack that had been made out of bottles and wood and straw and barrels and crates and fencing.

I picked up a stone and threw it. It smashed one of the bottle-windows. I chucked another one and it knocked over a pail. The third one hit a man square on the head.

"I'll leave your guts out for the dogs to chew on when I'm done with you!" he roared. As soon as he seen me, he raised his eyebrows.

My heart pounded. I quaked from toe to head.

There, in front of me, stood Turrety Knocks.

"I'm real sorry 'bout what happened to you," I yelled. "But my pa didn't start that fire!" My voice went away, came back, went away and came back again.

A crow flew up to a ledge above to see what all the fuss was 'bout.

Turrety Knocks coughed, which upset the crow. It flapped away.

"You let those boys get to you, didn't you?" he said.

Everything was hard to see 'cause my eyes went swimming.

Turrety Knocks set the pail upright.

"Don't go getting yourself worked up. I've got something for you."

Turrety Knocks disappeared into his shack, leaving the door wide open. I hesitated, in three minds 'bout what to do. What if Clem and the boys were waiting back there for me? I wiped my sleeve across my face and followed Turrety Knocks right on in.

My eyes took a while to adjust to the dark. I smelled earth and rock and mushrooms and damp wool and tobaccy and grass and wood smoke and sweet water. Dried herbs hung from the roof and green plants burst out of jam jars. He'd made a table out of an old whisky crate and chairs out of logs. Bottles glinted all around us in the gloom.

Turrety Knocks sat and waved for me to do the same.

I seen blue worms on the backs of his hands. Miss Ida showed us how to tell the age of a fallen tree by counting the rings on its stump. I wondered if I could work out Turrety Knocks's age by counting the lines on his face?

A breeze blew in through the window. Everything moved 'cause of the hole I'd made in it. Except for the rusty cat. It didn't move an ear.

"Sorry 'bout the window," I said.

"You're quick tempered, same as your pa," replied Turrety Knocks.

"You know Pa?"

"You're Twister, ain't you? I seen you in town with him a couple of times. I had him to thank for the job he gave me on the farm. I liked it there; he treated folks well."

I did not know Turrety Knocks had worked on the farm. When Pa hired help, the men would mostly be dots in the fields to me. Pa had warned me off speaking to them. He said that idle chatter kept them from doing their job. Ma said I should stay away from the men 'cause being a hard worker didn't always make you a good person. Whatever that meant.

I gawped at Turrety Knocks. I couldn't imagine Pa and him as friends. I'd got used to seeing him sucking hard on those brown bottles and pretending to be dead by the church. Sometimes he'd do that funny walk of his in town: two steps forward, two steps sideways and one step back. If he spoke, his words would be all sour with the liquor. And he'd talk real slow, as if he needed to be wound up with a key. But his words weren't sour today. Nor were they slow.

"Your pa is a fine man. That day of the fire in Holler Woods, he rushed over with the rest of us to try and put it out. I can tell you two things for certain 'bout him: he most definitely didn't start that fire and he must have had a mighty good reason to skip town 'cause his family ..." Turrety Knocks paused. If the clouds could have seen the look on his face right now, they'd rain tears for sure. He swallowed and continued on. "His family were everything to him and you can take that from someone who knows." Turrety Knocks's eyes were two different colours. Moss and bark.

"I'm sorry 'bout your wife and Lula," I said, quietly.

Turrety Knocks studied my face for a while. He nodded and looked away, his shoulders stooped with the weight of his grief.

I couldn't imagine how he must be feeling. Pa going

missing was hard enough. But the thought of never seeing him and Ma and Aunt Honey and Point again made my guts clench so tight, I thought I might puke.

Turrety Knocks rose from his seat and wrestled with a pile of junk by the window. The air sparkled with dust as he yanked out an envelope. I watched to see if the heap of trash might topple over, but it didn't. He came back and sat down. Took his time 'bout it too.

"Those boys ain't going to leave you alone."

My eyes found the dirt floor.

"And judging by my broken window, I'm guessing the situation's only going to get worse. They're trouble, Twister. You see the problem with Clem Hussable is he's only a boy, so nobody knows what he's capable of yet. But I can tell you Hack Hussable ain't the sort to mess with. He don't have one good bone in his body."

Thing is, I wasn't no scaredy-dog. I could hold my own 'cause it was in my blood. Aunt Honey said my ancestors came from Scotland and that they happened to be the toughest people in the world. Their eyes were the colour of mountains and they wore tartan kilts. Aunt Honey also said the Scots were awful smart and always handed their homework in on time.

I'd the whole weekend to figure out how to stop Clem from bothering me again. And figure it out I would 'cause on Monday, he'd want revenge for me biting him – sure as fleas made you itchy.

"I can take care of myself," I said, leaning back. I forgot I was perched on a log. I grabbed on to some ivy to stop myself from doing a backwards flip.

Turrety Knocks chose to ignore my circus-act ways. "Your pa asked me to give you this when the time was right."

"Pa?" I sat up straight as railings.

He nodded and handed me the envelope.

"You seen him?"

Turrety Knocks examined his hands, which were rough as fence posts. "The morning he vanished."

My heart sank into my boots. And then all the way down into the earth below.

"He asked if I'd look after the envelope for you, in case he ... well ... in case something should happen to him."

A silence filled the air. It near deafened me, so I decided to speak. "Was he in trouble?"

Turrety Knocks shook his head. "I can't tell you how sorry I am that I never asked him what was on his mind that day."

24

"What's inside it?" I said, holding up the envelope.

"That ain't none of my business, but I think the time is right for you to have it. If I can help in any way, you come and find me."

I heard Raging River flowing fast over the rocks.

The envelope must have been best friends with the sun 'cause it was faded. Pa had written my name across the front of it in pencil.

I felt tired and antsy, all at the same time. "Ma and Aunt Honey will be wondering where I am," I said. I shoved the envelope in my pocket and stood up to go.

"Here, take this. It's been nothing but a darn nuisance, cluttering the place up," muttered Turrety Knocks. He shuffled over to a pile of junk by the fire. He pulled out a parcel wrapped in newspaper and handed it to me.

I tore it open. Inside was my prize. My yellow kite.

"Done the best I could," he said.

Turrety Knocks must have found it in the churchyard. The frame had been straightened and fixed up with fishing wire. A long piece of string with rags on it replaced the tail that'd been torn off. It wouldn't win no beauty pageant, but it'd be good enough to fly.

"Thanks for the letter," I said. "And for mending my kite."

"Now be off with you before I tan your backside for smashing my window," Turrety Knocks growled as he shooed me out the door.

Up.

Up.

Up.

No time to avoid the stairs that grumbled.

I raced into my room and hid the kite in the wardrobe. I'd keep it as a surprise for Point. Him and me would fly it on Black Smoke Hill tomorrow. I stuck my hand in my pocket and pulled out an apple stalk and a white feather and a dried-up leaf and finally the envelope.

This was the best present I'd ever been given.

I sat down on the bed. It'd take me a while to pluck up the guts to open it. I wanted to savour the moment 'cause I'd never get the chance to wonder what was inside it again.

The second stair from the top creaked. Before I could move, the door flew open and Aunt Honey and Point swept in. The posters on my walls fluttered and the curtains lifted and the books clapped.

Point raced over and glued his wet nose to the envelope. He breathed in deep and puffed the air back out. His front paws stamped on the floor and his tail wagged so fast he nearly took off.

Had he picked up Pa's scent? Or was it the rusty cat he smelled?

I held the envelope away from his nose. If he sniffed it again, he might start woofing.

"You're late! Your ma is beside herself and you know fine well worrying takes it out of her. Supper's ready. What have you got there?" asked Aunt Honey.

"A letter from Miss Ida." I don't right know why I said this – it just fallen out of my mouth. I looked as guilty as a dog catched with its head in the cake tin.

"Twister! Is that a note to say you've been misbehaving

in class? And people wonder why my raven locks turned prematurely grey. Give it here."

"No!" I cried.

She snatched it out of my hand and tucked it into the pocket of her pinny.

"I'll deal with you later. Mercy me! You look like you've been running with a pack of wolves."

"Is Ma having dinner with us?"

"She's all tired out. It's just you and me tonight, so go and clean up." And with that Aunt Honey left.

Ma never ate with us any more. Sometimes it felt like she didn't even want to be in the same room as me. My eyes burned. I blinked the tears away. Point rested his chin on my knee. I scratched his neck. He closed his brown eyes, tilted his head to one side and opened his mouth. His breath felt warm against my leg.

That letter wasn't for Ma or Aunt Honey to see. Otherwise Pa would never have handed it to Turrety Knocks for safekeeping. I just had to think of a way to get it back 'cause it could lead me to where he was. And if I found him, Ma would go back to being her old self again and we'd all be happy.

*

"Twister, elbows off the table and stop playing with your food," scolded Aunt Honey.

I'd made mash-mountains and pea fields and a gravy river.

Before Pa left mealtimes had been noisy affairs. He would always tease Aunt Honey by asking her if there was a bachelor left in Culleroy who she hadn't kissed. Aunt Honey would shriek louder than a howloon bird and flush red roses. She'd say she'd rather smooch with a dung beetle than the likes of Herschel Poote or Spit Simmons. And Ma would laugh and tell the pair of them off for acting like a couple of kids in a schoolyard. Then we'd notice Point trying to sneak food from the table and Aunt Honey would end up chasing him out into the yard.

Now you could hear cutlery scraping off the plates and the kitchen clock ticking and Point yawning.

I sighed. How could I even eat when Pa's letter sat in Aunt Honey's pocket?

Aunt Honey sensed I was thinking 'bout her. "What's the matter? Cat got your tongue?"

That was funny 'cause Clem nearly had got my tongue today.

I flattened the mash-mountains with my fork. Aunt Honey gave me a look as if I was a steep hill she didn't have the energy to climb. "We ain't ever going to find you a husband with manners like those," she said. "Unless he comes from the travelling circus."

"I ain't getting married, that's for sissies," I said, squishing a pea.

Aunt Honey smiled. Lines came out from the sides of her eyes. She called them crow's feet. I reckoned they were so huge they could wear shoes. But I kept that thought to myself.

Point stuck his chin on the table. His eyes twinkled and his tongue lolled out the side of his mouth. The smell of the roasted chicken was driving him crazy la-la.

"Point, you *shooo* now! You've already been fed," said Aunt Honey. "I swear that dog would kill for chicken." She flapped her napkin in Point's face. He turned away from the table with a groan and slunk underneath it.

"I'm going into town tomorrow to drop off some eggs at the store. Want to come?" she asked.

"Me and Point are going exploring," I said.

"Twist, I'm wearing my knuckles to the bone trying to keep the farm going as it is. If you're not coming, you remember to do your chores before you go off gallivanting around," said Aunt Honey. "And don't stray far, you hear me?"

"I'll stick close by, Aunt Honey. I promise."

Mew the cat slunk in, ignoring me and Point and Aunt Honey. She even ignored the roasted chicken. But I betcha she'd tippy-toe back to sniff around when the moon woke up.

Aunt Honey sprinkled some pepper on to her mash. Point sneezed violently under the table giving us all a fright. Even Mew stopped licking her paw.

"Aunt Honey, did you know a man called Turrety Knocks who used to work on the farm?" I asked.

She sipped some water from her glass. "Yup."

"Do you know what happened to his wife and daughter?"

"Why you asking?" she said.

"I sit at Lula's old desk in class."

Aunt Honey stopped eating. Something that don't happen very often.

Aunt Honey dabbed at her mouth with her napkin. "We never told you 'bout the tragedy in Holler Woods. Your pa was worried it'd give you nightmares too. Then when he disappeared it slipped my mind to tell you. I'm sorry, Twist. I should have realized you'd find out 'bout it sooner or later."

I shrugged. "I felt dumb for not knowing, is all."

Aunt Honey cleared her throat. "Turrety Knocks was a good worker and a good man. Your pa had a lot of time for him. His wife's name was Bethy. She was a lovely lady: frail but kind and well mannered, unlike most of the folks around here. Their daughter, Lula, was charming: bright as a button and full of life. Your ma had even asked Bethy if she'd like to bring Lula over to play with you, but they never got the chance." Aunt Honey's words trailed off. "What happened to them is beyond comprehension, Twister." Aunt Honey shuddered. "Nature can be so cruel."

"You think it was a wild fire?"

"Absolutely. It'd been scorching hot and hadn't rained in weeks. Everything was like tinder. I said to your ma and pa we'd need to be extra vigilant around the farm. The conditions were perfect for a fire to rage out of control."

"You don't think it was started by a person?"

Two creases appeared on Aunt Honey's forehead.

"Ain't there something we can do for Turrety Knocks?" I said, changing the subject quickly.

"He's lost to the bottle right now, but we'll be here for him when he's ready to accept our help," said Aunt Honey. "People don't go looking for trouble, but it sure has a way of finding them. And talking 'bout trouble, do you want to explain to me what this is all 'bout?"

She took the brown envelope out from her pinny and waggled it in the air.

I held my breath.

The envelope slipped out of Aunt Honey's hand and fluttered down towards the ground. Point seen it. He leapt up and grabbed it. He sped off into the pantry with it firmly clenched between his teeth. Like the dog who'd got the cream.

I chased after him. Eating paper happened to be one of Point's most favourite things. Brown paper and newspaper and toilet paper and tissue paper and notepaper and birthday paper and Christmas paper and wallpaper. Even baking paper. He'd happily munch it all.

"Point, no!" I shouted. The thought of never reading Pa's letter was too awful to think 'bout.

Point started to shred the envelope.

I picked up a freshly baked scone from the rack and tossed it to him. As he catched it between his jaws, the envelope fallen out of his mouth. He wagged his tail as I snatched it away from him. It shone with dog slobber and a big chunk had been torn off the side of it. I sure as heck hoped I could still read Pa's words. I folded it up and tucked it into my pocket.

I stomped out of the pantry and flung myself on to my chair.

"Point ate the letter," I muttered.

"Oh no! Go on – tell me the worst. What had Miss Ida written in it?" asked Aunt Honey.

"Miss Ida wanted you to know I'd won the boat-building competition at school." I'd be sure to end up in that fiery place I'd heard 'bout where bad people went for fibbing.

Aunt Honey's forkful of chicken froze mid-air. "Why! You should've said something! Here was me thinking you'd got into trouble in class."

"You didn't give me a chance to explain myself," I said.

Aunt Honey squirmed on her chair before wolfing down the chicken. "Point swallowed the whole thing?" she asked with her mouth full.

"Uh-huh," I said. My face burned with the lie.

"That dog would steal candy from a child," said Aunt Honey, all exasperated. "And then eat the child."

"I've still got my prize."

"Well, I guess it's the winning that counts, not the piece of paper that says you've won," said Aunt Honey. "What did you get?"

"A yellow kite."

"Now I know why you don't want to come into town with me tomorrow!" laughed Aunt Honey. "Well, a rousing ramble in the fresh air will do you good after working so hard all week at school." She cleared the plates away from the table. "Wait till I tell your ma the good news. It'll cheer her up no end."

"I wish she'd come down and eat with us," I said.

Aunt Honey patted my shoulder. "All she needs is a bit of space to work things out right now. Be patient and you'll see time is a great healer."

She proceeded to clatter around the kitchen. "I baked a chocolate fudge cake. Reckon you could do with an extra big slice, seeing as you're the first person in the family to win a prize for building a boat."

Aunt Honey's cakes were delicious. And some.

"Aunt Honey, do you think trees can talk?" I asked.

"What goes on inside that head of yours?" she said. "I think our hopes of a circus man taking you off our hands may be a touch on the optimistic side." Aunt Honey placed the glossy chocolate fudge cake on the table. "Now then, would you like some fresh cream with it?"

Point scooted out from the pantry. He wagged his tail and woofed at Aunt Honey, all expectantly.

I waited until the moon peeked in through the window
and the house went quiet. Except for Aunt Honey's snoring,
that was. She sounded much the same as Swayback, our
prize hog.

I tippy-toed over to the baldy rug. I pulled it back and
lifted up the creaky floorboard. I'd thought it wise to hide
the envelope where it'd be safe as barns. I grabbed it and
hurried back to bed.

Point lay fast asleep across the door, his paws
twitching. I betcha he was dreaming 'bout chasing rabbits
on Black Smoke Hill. He loved chasing rabbits on Black

Smoke Hill. And tearing paper and chewing his red squeaky ball and scoffing roasted chicken.

My finger traced over my name on the envelope. Frogs flop-flipped in my belly: I hoped whatever was inside it would tell me where Pa really was. If Point and me found him tomorrow, we could bring him straight home. Ma'd get better in no time. And then she'd take me out of school so we could read stories under the trees and I'd never have to see Clem Hussable or those awful girls ever again.

I steadied my hands. Careful as careful could be, I opened the envelope. Inside was a letter. I pulled it out: the paper was as fragile as butterfly wings. Point had taken a huge chunk out of it. But I could still read some of the words. One thing was for sure, Miss Ida would've given Pa ten out of ten and a gold star for his handwriting.

My Dearest Twister,

I'm sorry to have to say that if you are readin[g]

chance that I am no longer alive. This is impo[rtant]

approached by a lady called Maymay – stay away fr[om]

she'll say belongs to you.

Whatever you do, and I can't stre[ss]

Don't take it! Your life depends on it.

Look after Ma and Aunt Honey. It'l[l]

help out where you can.

Forgive me for not being there to

Most of all, be happy my beautifu[l]

I will never stop loving you.

Pa

I read the letter again. And again. And again.

I read it until my eyes stung.

Had something happened to Pa? Who was this lady he mentioned? And what did my life depend on not taking?

I pressed the paper against my face and closed my eyes. It smelled of dust and soap and lemon and pepper and spice. The same as Pa's clothes done in the closet.

41

The moon reached in through the window to touch Point. His black fur turned into a gleaming coat of silvery beams.

Aunt Honey said it was easy being a kid and hard being a grown-up. But it felt like the other way around right now.

There was only one thing I knew for sure. If I found this Maymay, she might be able to tell me what'd happened to Pa.

Somewhere in the distance a hooty-owl screeched.

The next morning, I woke to find Point standing beside the bed with the red squeaky ball in his mouth. His eyes were as brown as june bugs but there was a deep blue in them too. They were as beautiful as beautiful can be.

Point dropped the ball and yawned in my face. Every bit of his body wagged, as if he hadn't seen me in years.

I reached out to clap his side. "Point, we'll go snickerbug hunting and you can bring your ball too," I said. "But it's going to have to be later 'cause I got chores to do first."

He glanced at me all huffy before he threw himself down and put his head on his paws. His back leg kicked out behind him, rumpling up the baldy rug. He pretended to snooze as I threw on shorts and a T-shirt.

I thought 'bout Pa's letter. My heart stretched with crazy joy that I'd read his words. It was like he'd finally spoken to me after months of silence. My guts clenched some 'cause of his warning. But I'd have to find this Maymay. Nobody knew what had happened to him: not Ma, not Aunt Honey, not Sheriff Buckstaffy, not Doc Winters, not the folks of Culleroy. Not even Turrety Knocks. Maymay might be the only person with answers.

Aunt Honey had already left for Culleroy. I found a note on the kitchen table, which thankfully Point had decided not to eat.

Twister,

   Sandwiches in the pantry – help yourself. Don't pester your ma or climb any trees or stray too far from the farm or be talking to any strangers. Stay away from Raging River! I'll be back by four.

   Aunt Honey x

   PS Remember your chores.

I grabbed an apple and headed out into the yard. I

loved the sound of biting into one: all crisp and delicious. It was one of my most favourite noises. That and bacon sizzling in a pan. I could listen to that for ever 'cause it made my ears happy.

I stopped by the chicken coop first. Gorgeous George the rooster and Peckers the hen had fallen out. Feathers were scattered everywhere. The other hens clucked 'bout it in the corner.

I let them out and Gorgeous George flapped straight up on to the top of the coop. He always done this. Aunt Honey said it was so he could attract the attention of the hens. She said Gorgeous George and Pert Gumshoe from the garage had a lot in common on account of the fact they both strutted around if there was a lady present.

I collected a whole basket of eggs without breaking any. There were so many, Aunt Honey might bake another cake.

I checked on the hogs. Old Swayback stuck his snout out through the fence and wiggled it. He loved it when you scratched his ears. Some people thought hogs were stupid. But I know for a fact they were a whole lot smarter than the folks who thought this. None of the other hogs were looking, so I gave Swayback the rest of my apple. He closed his eyes at the sheer joy of its sweetness.

The hogs and I always played the same game. I chased them while trying to rake out their old straw. And then they chased me when they seen I had food scraps. I poured fresh water into the trough and chucked the rest of it on to the soil, so they could take a mud bath later. Though Swayback was a mighty prissy hog. He wouldn't take a bath if he thought folks were watching.

I looked in on our cows, Merle and Gloria. Aunt Honey said they were highly strung but I'd never seen any strings on them. I hurried past the barn and the vegetable patch on the way up to Proudfoot's field. He galloped over, shaking his mane and flicking his tail. He can be a real windy horse in the mornings, especially after eating oats. Sometimes he'd fart when he was trotting. That made Pa and me laugh. Aunt Honey said ladies didn't find flatulence amusing. But I knew for a fact she did if she thought no one was around.

I loved the way Proudfoot made his skin shiver if a buzzy-fly landed on it. I wish I could do that. I've practised enough times. But I always ended up shaking my whole arm or leg. Buzzy-flies were real annoying, especially the noise they made. I hated it when they landed on my food. It upset me 'cause I knew what they landed on in the farm and it ain't pretty.

Proudfoot always snorted on my head. It was his way of saying *hello*. As soon as he done that, he'd be at my pocket. He knew I had a carrot for him; I always had a carrot for him. Pa said Proudfoot ate so many carrots, he was surprised he wasn't orange and that he didn't get chased by the rabbits.

A movement at the house caught my eye. Ma was gazing out of the bedroom window. I waved at her but she turned away. My shoulders slumped. With Pa gone it felt as though Ma couldn't see me no more. The sooner I could find this Maymay and bring Pa home, the better.

I ran down to the yard. Point sat up and thumped his tail in the dust. I ruffled his fur and he licked my hand. He always stopped my thoughts from getting too sad.

I fetched my bag and raced upstairs to grab my kite.

When I reappeared, Point wagged his tail, all slow. He knew something was going to happen. But he wasn't getting too excited 'bout it until he knew what for sure.

"Come on then, fearless hound! Let's go!" I said. I sometimes called him that 'cause Point ain't scared of nothing. Well, except for getting his coat clipped at the Poochy Parlour. That made him quake like a jelly on a drum.

Point skidded to a halt at the gate, waiting for me to open it. He snuffled at the kite and then pushed past me, almost tripping me up. He bolted to the end of the path and glanced back. Like I was the tortoise and he was the hare.

Climbing Black Smoke Hill sure was hard work. But the birds sang and the flowers jiggled and the crickets jumped 'cause the grass tickled them. Even the crows were cheerful. They strutted around, showing off their black-diamond feathers.

I couldn't stop thinking 'bout Pa's letter. And Maymay. Finding her could be like trying to spot a white mouse in a field of snow. If Maymay came from around these parts, Aunt Honey might know her 'cause Aunt Honey knew everybody. Thing is, she'd want to know why I wanted to know. And that was where it could get tricky. Another thing niggled at me. If Pa said I was to stay away from her, did this mean she was bad? What if Maymay was a witch? I'd heard the other girls in class whispering 'bout witches. They said they were all warts and dirty looks and curses and hissy black cats and spells. I didn't want to go messing with no witches. I'd be sure to say the wrong thing and end up being turned into a bumpy toad. Or something like that.

I spied a clearing up ahead. Happy news for my aching limbs 'cause it meant we'd finally reached the top of Black Smoke Hill.

The view took my breath away. From here you could see the farm and Raging River and Cedar Creek Lake and the school and the church and all the houses in Culleroy. The heat made the mighty Misty Peak mountains shimmer in the distance. Bird song floated up from the valley. I smelled the breath of the forest: all sticky pine and baked herbs and wild flowers and hot grass. Insects hummed and rattled and zizzied; bees gathered on giant bushes of yellow flowers as if they were dropping into their local diner for pollen shakes; ants marched and lizards flicked their tails and butterflies flashed their patterned wings.

I placed the kite on the ground and unravelled the string. Point came over to sniff it. He whined.

"You're going to love this," I said.

He woofed. I laughed and started running across the

grass, Point bounding alongside me. I let the string out and the kite rose up into the air. He tried to catch its tail, but a gust of wind lifted it out of reach and it flew above us like a giant yellow bird. Point kicked his heels up and raced round and round and round, his tongue flapping out the side of his mouth. It looked very much as if he was trying to fly it.

We came to a halt at the edge of the hill. Point threw himself down on the grass, panting. But his eyes never left the yellow kite, not once.

I let the string full out. You could no longer see the bent frame or guess that the tail was made from rags. It was beautiful in the sky: it was the best prize ever.

Point and me headed down towards Cedar Creek Lake. Aunt Honey said I'd have to help around the farm tomorrow. So, I thought it best to collect the snickerbugs for Miss Ida while I was here. When she seen them on Monday, I'd be sure to get back into her good books.

Snickerbugs can only be catched between spring and summer. Each one had two weeks to go 'bout its business before it died. That made me sad. Aunt Honey said it was a short life but they shone bright. She said there wasn't nothing greater in life than shining bright.

I loved snickerbugs. If you stroked their backs, they made a noise as if they were snickering. They only came out at night and when they did they glowed brighter than the stars. I knew they were only bugs and all, but I thought they were like precious jewels for the trees and land to wear.

When we reached Cedar Creek Lake, a light ripple moved across the water towards us. As if Mew had stuck her paw in on the other side.

Point splish-splashed right on in to cool off. His black ears fallen over his eyes as he gazed at the strange green world underneath the surface.

There was an island in the middle of the lake. It was overgrown with bent trees and dark plants and twisted vines and knotted weeds. One day I'd build my own boat for real and Point and me would sail over to it. Then we'd find the X and dig for treasure. There just had to be treasure buried on an island like that.

I took out my lunchbox. Snickerbugs hated the daylight, so they hid in the bark of old crumbly trees until the moon showed up.

I found a black oak laying down a few yards from the

lake and interrupted a line of ants peeling back the bark. Under it, I found two snickerbugs fast asleep. I popped them into the box and put them in my bag so the sunlight wouldn't disturb them.

I walked over to the edge of Cedar Creek Lake. A soft breeze tickled my skin. Waves curled and swished flat and insects rushed home and birds rejoiced. Fish gulped and vines tightened and flowers slowly closed. Being here made me forget just how wretched life had become without Pa. It was tempting to stay and watch the water turn from gold to pink, but I'd made up my mind. I was going to ask Aunt Honey if she knew who Maymay was.

The thought of it made my guts twinge.

I whistled to Point. He crashed out of the undergrowth wearing a twig hat and bright green sticky-willy earrings. I snorted. Point barked and shook himself. And with that, we began to wind our way home.

The kitchen smelled of baked ham and warm apples and buttery potatoes and green, greener than green beans.

"There you are! I'd the best day, Twist. Hec Bartle bought all of our eggs and he's placed a huge order for some more of your ma's strawberry jam. He said the last lot practically flew off the shelves. And guess what? The Goodwill Home of Tranquillity is interested in your ma supplying their jam too. Guess jam's not too much of a challenge for old folks with no teeth."

"That's great news, Aunt Honey," I said.

Mew sat on top of the cabinet. She yawned, stretched

and shook herself. She opened her marmalade eyes to watch the ham.

"Had an ice-cream float at the Fountain. Three scoops too 'cause your ma wasn't there to keep me in check. Purely medicinal, of course, to prevent me from getting heat stroke," said Aunt Honey, chucking the steaming beans into a bowl and adding a huge dollop of butter. "Go on, sit."

There were three places set at the table. Ma must be dining with us tonight! I smiled and grabbed the water jug. I filled all the glasses, careful not to spill a drop.

"Oh – your ma's just gone for a lie down. She managed out to the vegetable patch for an hour or two, but I think the heat got the better of her," said Aunt Honey.

"We could eat real fast so she wouldn't have to sit with us for long?"

"You know that'd give me terrible wind, but it was sweet of you to suggest. Your ma'll take her supper upstairs later."

Aunt Honey seen the look on my face. "It's good she's resting up 'cause tomorrow she'll have all the energy she needs to make more jam," she said, plonking the beans on the table.

I looked down at my plate.

Aunt Honey brightened up her voice. "Hey, I got you a present."

"You did?"

"Shooglepopple candy seeing as you won the boat-building competition," she said.

"Thanks."

"You can have some after supper," said Aunt Honey. "Here – help yourself to mashed potato." She handed me the bowl. "Hey, slow down there, Twist. What did you get up to today that's made you so ravenous?"

"My chores like you asked. And Point and I catched some snickerbugs for Miss Ida down by Cedar Creek Lake."

"If I so much as find one of them bugs glowing in my bed tonight, you and your critters can take up residency in the barn."

"Don't worry, Aunt Honey, they're in an empty fish bowl – and before you ask, there's a lid on it; and yes, I've fed them."

Aunt Honey waggled her fork at me. "I told you to stay near the farm. Your ma won't be best pleased you were at the lake."

"I'm a good swimmer. You're always saying you wouldn't be surprised if I had gills or webbed feet."

"Cedar Creek Lake is an isolated spot, Twist. I think she's more concerned 'bout who you might bump into up there," said Aunt Honey. "As am I."

I shovelled a fork full of mash into my mouth and stared at her.

"Something on your mind?" she asked.

"Havsh shou heardsh osh a lashy by she mame ogh MayhMayh?" I said, as casually as I could.

"Want to swallow your food and try that again?"

The time had come. It was now or never.

"Have you ever heard of a lady by the name of Maymay?" I asked.

Aunt Honey piled a heap of mash and ham and beans on to her fork. "It never ceases to amaze me the questions you ask." She shovelled it into her mouth in one go. Aunt Honey always ate as if she'd win a prize for being the first to clear her plate.

"Some of the girls were talking 'bout her in class," I fibbed. My cheeks turned the same colour as rhubarb stalks.

"That's good you're making friends, Twist," beamed Aunt Honey.

Truth is, Cherry had told the others I sat on a chair

that was cursed. None of them would come near me during break time.

"Maymay. Sheesh. I've not heard her name in a while," she said.

"You know her?" I said, trying not to sound too excited.

"She was a medicine woman who lived in Holler Woods. Dolly Prebble went to see her a few years back 'bout her knees 'cause she couldn't afford to see Doc Winters. Maymay fixed them up good and proper by all accounts."

"What's a medicine woman?"

Aunt Honey sawed at her ham. "There was a time when doctors and pharmacies didn't exist in Culleroy. This meant if people fallen ill they had to cure themselves with natural remedies. A medicine woman knew all the local plants, herbs and roots that could heal people."

"How did they know what to use?"

"The knowledge would have been passed down from generation to generation. See the mint we've got growing out the back? Your grandma taught us that if you mix it with hot water it's just 'bout the best thing you can settle an upset stomach with."

"Maybe we should give some to Proudfoot, he was real windy this morning," I said.

"I'm not sure there's enough in the whole of Culleroy to cure him," said Aunt Honey.

My heart skipped around my chest. "Do you know where Maymay lives?"

"I think Dolly mentioned her cabin was somewhere near Juniper Falls." Aunt Honey's eyes shone. Her voice dropped to an excited whisper. "And get this, Dolly also said Maymay could speak with the dead."

Point chose at that very moment to lick my hand. I leapt up, making Aunt Honey cry out. Mew the cat jumped down from the cabinet and shot out of the room. Point wagged his tail, wondering what all the fuss was 'bout.

"Is that true?" I asked, "'bout her talking to the dead?" I settled back down in my chair.

"Heck, I don't know. Dolly swore blind it was."

"Wouldn't that make her more of a witch?"

"I tell you something, Twist. You wouldn't catch me going into Holler Woods at night looking for her help."

"She don't see people during the day?"

"Dolly told me she had to find her cabin when the

moon was full and take her a gift, otherwise Maymay would have turned her away."

"*Really?*"

"Uh-huh. Dolly's pink coat never recovered. It's still got marks on it from when she fallen on her backside in the mud," sniffed Aunt Honey. "Which reminds me, I seen Turrety Knocks in town impersonating a sack of potatoes. That old coot's been at the liquor again."

I scratched my nose. He'd been fine yesterday. I sure hoped me hitting him on the head with a stone hadn't made him turn to the drink again.

"I'll drop off a food parcel for him tomorrow and check he's OK. If he's been on the bottle I dare say he won't have eaten," said Aunt Honey.

I thought of my kite he'd mended and how heavenly it'd looked flying in the sky. "I could take it to him?"

"That's a kind offer, Twist, but your ma's going to need help picking strawberries tomorrow. I can't bend down in this girdle of mine."

"Remember when you were picking peas for three days in a row last year? Pa said we'd need to borrow Hooper Clank's hammer and anvil to straighten you out."

Aunt Honey hooted. "The cheek of that man!"

I looked over at his empty seat. The smile faded from my face. My heart cracked with the pain of missing him. "Aunt Honey?"

"Mmmm?"

"Did I do something wrong? That why he left?"

"Oh, Twister! Nothing could be further from the truth. He loves you and your ma very much. We're all going to have to stay strong, and trust in our hearts that one day he will come back to us. I tell you what you need, some of my apple pie and custard. It's sunshine in a bowl, I tell you. Sunshine in a bowl."

What I really needed was to ask Maymay 'bout Pa. Except, I couldn't right tell Aunt Honey that.

After helping Aunt Honey with the dishes, I climbed the stairs to my room. The good news was Maymay might live somewhere near Juniper Falls. The bad news was I'd have to find her at night. In the dark. With all them critters with the fur and the teeth and the glinting eyes and the claws.

An invisible hand squeezed my guts. Hard.

I sat on my bed. I wanted to crawl into it and pull the

covers over my head, just like Ma. But that would be of no use to nobody.

I kicked Point's ball. It thudded against the wall and hurried back to me.

Aunt Honey seemed to think Pa would come back in his own good time. But what if he was lying somewhere injured, praying someone would show up? I didn't want to wait any longer. I had a *real* chance to find him. And if I didn't grab it, I knew I'd never ever forgive myself.

The fat moon squeezed itself into my window. Its light blinded the stars and chased away the dark. There would be no better time to go to Maymay's than tonight. My pulse quickened at the thought and my mouth watered. I felt sick.

Aunt Honey said the best way to stop yourself from feeling fear was to be present in the now. She said if you quit worrying 'bout what might happen and concentrate on what *was* happening right at this very moment in time, fear disappeared.

I decided to give it a go. Packing a bag would take my mind off things. I figured a torch would be a good idea, in case the moon took fright too and hid behind some clouds. And my penknife might come in handy if

Maymay got all sassy. Besides, there was no telling what could be lurking in them woods tonight.

Aunt Honey had mentioned Dolly had to give Maymay a gift. And I'm guessing a bunch of buttercups wouldn't cut it. It would most likely have to be something that was precious to me. There were Pa's old books. I missed him reading to me 'bout pirates and insects and birds and skeletons and kings and knights and castles and angels and dragons. The books were worn around the edges. I guess Pa had loved them as well and that made them way too precious to hand over to an old witch.

I looked at my pebble animals and my shells and the snickerbugs. Then I spotted my prize on the floor. My beautiful yellow kite. Me and Point had the best time ever flying it today. I'd hate to lose it again which meant it'd be the perfect gift to give to Maymay.

Aunt Honey was right. Fear did go if you stopped thinking 'bout it.

The trees in Holler Woods weren't so friendly at night: some of them looked like they were screaming. And the place didn't sound too welcoming neither. There was grunting and squawking and clawing and creaking and scuttling. And howling and clicking and gnawing and slithering and croaking.

Ma and Aunt Honey would have my garters for guts if they knew we'd sneaked out. Point snuffled at a twisty tree, which had scratch marks on its trunk. I didn't want to go thinking 'bout what'd done that 'cause it ain't no kitten.

I closed my eyes and thought 'bout Pa. One of the last times we'd spoken was in the orchard. He'd catched an orange and brown coloured bug and showed it to me.

"What's this called?" he'd asked.

"A bark weevil," I'd said.

"They're one of the few insects that play dead if they think their life is in danger," Pa had said. "Ain't it incredible how a tiny thing like this knows how to keep itself safe from predators?"

I'd studied the insect. It lay perfectly still in the palm of Pa's hand, with its legs in the air.

"He should be in the films 'cause his acting skills sure are good," I'd said.

Pa had laughed. "We'd better let him go, just in case he's got a screen test later on." He'd bent down to return the insect to the leaves. The sun had catched his eyes making them sparkle blue, bluer-than-blue.

I blinked and found myself back in the woods. My heart had opened up wide. All I wanted was Pa home. And I had to believe Maymay would help me find him.

I took a deep breath, until my lungs stretched tight, and stepped forward. My footsteps sounded awful loud. I remembered what Pa had told me 'bout brown bears.

He said it was best to announce your arrival, that way you wouldn't go giving them no surprises. Bears didn't appreciate surprises much.

The full moon shone in the black velvet sky. All the trees and plants were silver, as if Hooper Clank had made them in his smithy. Spider webs shimmered and fluttery moths gleamed and milky bats skimmed over our heads. Fireflies and snickerbugs lit up the path like teeny-tiny fancy tea lights.

Point went on ahead, but not by much. He'd stop with his ears up and glance around so fast his cheeks flapped. I guess he was wondering if we should be here too.

I halted every time Point did. His tail stiffened and he'd lift his front paw in the air. I thought it best to let him decide when it was OK to move off again.

There was a whole load of thoughts I was trying not to think 'bout. But the harder I tried not to think 'bout them, the more I did. What else was in here with us? Was Maymay dangerous? Would Point and me get lost? And what if thinking bad thoughts actually made them happen?

I recognized the old oak tree to the left of the path. When you stood next to it you felt the same size as an ant. Most of the folks in Culleroy had carved their names on the trunk at one time or another. Someone had even scratched *White Eye will get you* on it. As if. I reckon Clem Hussable had done that. His pa must have scared him senseless with the tales 'bout White Eye coming to steal his soul if he didn't behave. You'd think there was enough bad stuff going on in the world without having to make stuff up. If I was Clem I'd be way more frightened of Hack Hussable 'cause he was the real monster.

A bush next to the tree shook, making my heart bounce around my ribcage. Something was behind it that sounded way bigger than the bush.

I brought out my penknife, but it'd be as useful as a toothpick against a ferocious animal. The leaves rustled again. Before I could yell, a deer shot out, bounding off into the darkness. Then everything fell silent.

I let my breath out and laughed. I done that when I got real nervous. Point stared at me: he thought I was lally-doo. He snapped his jaws shut and walked on. I stopped snorting; no way did I want to be left here on my own.

Up.

Up.

Up we climbed. I reckoned walking in the dark made a journey seem seven hundred times as long. I leant against a leaning tree to catch my breath. The hairs rose on the backs of my arms and my skin crawled. I couldn't shake the feeling we weren't alone. If I was in the kitchen and Ma was in her room, I'd still know she was there. I could sense her. The same way I could sense something or someone with us now.

The air filled with expectation. It reminded me of waiting for the dusty sheet to go up at the church play.

Twigs snapped. Was it another deer?

I turned around, slowly. My eyes peered into the gloom.

Point gave a warning woof. He growled fierce and tore off, crashing through the bushes. Then he let out a high-pitched yelp.

The whole of Holler Woods held its breath. I *ran*.

Branches raked at my face and roots tripped me up and thorns slashed my legs and nettles stung my skin.

My breath was raspy-gaspy. My heart tried to kick its way out of my chest.

"Point!" I shouted. "Point!"

A bird screeched. I pursed my lips together and whistled.

Nothing.

I threw the kite down and brought out the torch. If he was on the ground his eyes would gleam in its beam. I clicked it on and swung it round. I seen big eyes and small eyes glinting, but not Point's eyes. The jiggling light made everything even bigger and darker. It felt as if Holler Woods was closing in on me.

My head banged and my eyes smarted and my throat tightened. It was my fault Point was missing. I should never have brought him.

I wiped the sweat off my face with my sleeve.

"Point!" I shouted his name one last time. But only the sounds of the woods reached my ears. He must have run off after something which meant he could be anywhere by now.

I grabbed my kite and scrambled back up towards the path. It didn't make no sense going home. Ma and Aunt Honey wouldn't be able to find Point neither. They'd just yell at me for being stupid and keep me locked indoors for the rest of my life.

Chances are he'd get fed up and turn tail. Point had

the finest nose in all of Culleroy. If he came back to this spot, he'd catch my scent for sure and follow me to Maymay's.

I marched up the path. Anger at losing Point filled my body. It left no room for any other feelings. I no longer jumped when the trees clacked together and twigs broke. If a bear dared to growl at me, I'd roar back in its face five times as loud. And if Maymay was mean? Why! I'd just kick her on the shin!

My jaw clenched tight. My teeth hurt. Sweat trickled down my back. I pushed through some thick bushes and stumbled out the other side.

My ears filled with the mighty swoosh of water tumbling over rocks into a pool. I'd made it to Juniper Falls! I had never seen Juniper Falls at night before. The water bubbled and frothed and sparkled. A mist rose up in an arc above it and glowed in the sky. I've seen plenty of rainbows but I ain't never seen no moonbow before.

I walked over to the side of the pool and knelt down. Frogs creaked and cicadas rattled and spiders drummed and fish splish-splashed. I placed the kite beside me. What'd I been thinking coming here in the middle of the night? I was as mad as bats. And some.

I scooped some water up in my hands. It tasted cool and fresh and sweet.

I seen my reflection quivering on the surface of the pool. That was when I noticed a pale face rippling on the water, right next to mine.

10

I cried out and fallen into the pool.

Down.

Down.

Down, I sank into its blackness. Water filled my ears until everything had gone quiet. The cold made my skin jingle-jangle. My breath escaped out my mouth in bubbles.

A slimy weed wrapped itself around my leg and held on tight. I thrashed around and kicked it off. My legs stretched downwards until my feet hit the slippery stones at the bottom. I pushed with all my might.

Up.

Up.

Up.

I shot through the surface of the pool and gulped in the night air. Filling my lungs until they near burst had never felt so good. That was when I seen a girl standing at the water's edge.

"Hell's bells," I yelled, swimming over to the rocks. "Has nobody told you it ain't polite sneaking up on people?" I dragged myself out on to the grass. My clothes were darker and stuck to me. I'd two skins now.

"Hello!" she said, cheerily.

I shook my head. Hundreds of moon-filled droplets flew through the air.

I glared at her. She must have been out in the woods for a while 'cause she was covered toe-to-head in dirt. Her dress had frills on it. I'm guessing at one time it must have been white. It was the kinda dress that'd make me itch. I wouldn't be seen alive in a thing like that. "You scared me whole to death," I snapped. "What were you thinking?"

Her smile vanished and she wrung her hands together. "I . . . I was just pleased to see you. It ain't often you find a girl in Holler Woods at this time of night. Most of them are tucked up in bed." Now she looked all sorry. But not for me – for herself. Her bottom lip trembled and her eyes scrunched up.

Oh lordy! There wasn't nothing worse than a crybaby.

I emptied half of the pool out my boots. "What the blazes are you doing creeping around here anyhow?" I asked.

She un-scrunched her eyes. "I live here."

"I ain't never seen you before." I pulled a long piece of green weed out of my hair. "Where do you go to school?"

"Ma teaches me at home."

"My ma used to do the same but now I go to the school in Culleroy. I don't like it there much."

"Do you know Cherry Bonnwell?"

"Sure do, but she don't want to know me."

"Sounds like Cherry all right." The girl squinted at me. "I'm sure I've seen you before. Do you have a dog?"

My guts tied themselves in knots. "I usually do but I lost him tonight 'cause he chased after something. His name's Point."

"Maybe it was a ghost," she said.

"There ghosts in here?" I asked.

"It's a favourite haunt." She smiled at me. "I'm real sorry I scared you."

She wasn't like the other girls at school. They'd have ignored me. Or Cherry would have called me something Aunt Honey wouldn't care for me repeating. Even though she was annoying and made me fall into the pool and wore a frilly dress, I was sure glad of her company. "Ain't you worried you might bump into a bear? Or witch?" I whispered, in case there were any bears or witches listening in.

She tilted her head. "There are worse things in these woods." The way she said it made chicken-bumps pop up on my arms. "Where do you live?"

"Four Winds Farm by Raging River. Why you asking?"

"So I know where to take your dog if I find him."

"Thanks," I said, staring at her. Her long hair was the same colour as church pews. Her skin glowed pale as teeth, except for where the dirt was.

"You've got mud on your cheek," I said.

She plain ignored me. "Wotcha doing here?" she asked.

"Looking for someone."

"Maybe I can help," she said. "Who you looking for?"

"A lady called Maymay."

The girl grinned and clapped her hands. "Everyone knows Maymay. Her cabin is over there." She pointed to the trees opposite the pool.

"Say, is she a witch?" I asked.

"Holler Woods is full of them, I can tell you." The girl stepped forward. "*Love* the kite."

"It's a beauty, ain't it?"

"Can I fly it?"

"It's a present for Maymay – but if she don't want it you can."

"My pa made me a kite but it got stuck in a tree." The girl hopped from one foot to the other. "What you seeing Maymay for?"

"I'm looking for someone," I said.

"Who?"

"My pa."

"You lost your dog *and* your pa?" she asked.

I snorted. And 'cause I snorted, she snorted too. "I didn't lose Pa – he disappeared. I think Maymay might know what happened to him."

"What's he like? If he was here, I might have seen

him," she said, flicking her hair back with her hand. Some flecks of dirt fallen on to her white dress. Her ma would tan her backside when she got home. Her frock was as good as ruined.

"Pa's tall with blue, bluer-than-blue eyes and his hair's the colour of snow. He's kind to animals and really funny. His favourite bird is the golden eagle. And another thing, he prefers his pancakes on the well-fired side. I like mine the same way."

"I don't like burnt things much," she said, flatly. "Nah! He's not here – I'd have remembered him." She puffed her fringe out of her eyes. "Sometimes my pa goes missing too and there ain't nothing I can do 'bout it neither."

What were the chances of that? Meeting a girl who knew what it was like to have a vanishing pa. Before I could ask her name, something moved in the trees behind us.

Her hand shot out to grab my wrist. She ought to have put a vest on 'cause she felt as cold as iron bars. She whispered urgently. "You should go. See the fork in the path? Take the one on the right. Keep on it until you see a pond. It's hidden by trees, so listen out for wind chimes; Maymay's cabin is there."

"Thanks, but what if that's my dog?" I said, trying to peer over her shoulder.

"It ain't no dog. Now hurry."

I snatched the kite and my bag. My boots squelched as I ran towards the path. I looked back but the girl had gone. Strange thing was, I missed her already.

After the brightness of the moon on the water, my eyes had to make friends with the dark again. I hurried along the path deeper into the woods. The trees groaned and creaked and whined. They weren't too happy 'bout me disturbing their beauty sleep.

A low moaning noise silenced them. I whirled round. And hurt my ears trying to hear it again. That was when I spotted a black shape heading towards me. It snuffled and huffed and slobbered and snorted.

Pa told me never to run from a bear. Bears might fool you into thinking they were clumsy and all. But they were way faster than a cat being chased by a dog. Pa also said I should never hide from one up a tree. Bears were far better at climbing on account of their paws. Pankery Hope brought a bear claw into class for his show-and-tell. It reminded me of a brown glossy meat hook.

I slipped behind a tree and sank down on to my knees. I hoped the wind wouldn't waft my scent straight to its twitching nose, otherwise it'd know exactly what I was. Dinner.

I closed my eyes and lifted the kite over my head. The bear took a few more steps forward and sniffed the ground. It must have found a beetle or a frog 'cause it chewed on something.

The bear smelled the air. And I smelled it. All pine sap and sour berries and dock leaves and musk and honeybee and puddles and damp fur and creeper roots.

I remembered the bark weevil Pa had found in the orchard. He'd said it played dead when it was in danger. I wished I could do that right now. But I knew a bear wouldn't be so easy to fool. I wanted to think 'bout how I could scare it away. But all that came to mind were Pa and Ma and Aunt Honey and Point and Turrety Knocks.

The bear bellowed from the depths of its guts.

I shrank to the size of a piece of grit.

Two small higher-pitched cries answered the bear's call. She must have baby bears!

The tree trembled. I lifted the kite and seen the bear's huge paws above me, either side of the trunk.

My lungs stopped working.

The bear scratched the tree, her nails slicing through the wood. Bark rain showered down on me. She let go and thudded on to the ground. I waited to feel her hot breath on the top of my skull, but nothing happened. I peeped out from behind the kite.

Two weeny-teeny eyes stared at me. One of the bear cubs had snuck round the side of the tree. It looked much like Pearl Wiggle had given it a shampoo and set 'cause its brown fur was all puffed up. The cub grabbed the kite tail and tugged on it.

Pa warned me never to come between a bear and its babies. I couldn't right shoo it away 'cause I'd attract the attention of Ma bear. I flapped my free arm silently in the air to scare it off. The baby bear's eyes sparkled. This game sure did beat chewing on its ma's ears. It yanked even harder on the tail. I held on to the kite for dear life.

Ma bear cried out. I waved my arm faster. The little cub tugged one more time and the tail ripped clean off. It trotted away with the string trailing behind it. As if it'd just won a prize at the fair.

I let my breath out and waited until everything went

quiet. Thing was, which way should I go? Home? Or deeper into Holler Woods?

I'd lost my dog and nearly lost my life and now I was just plain lost.

I picked the kite up and rested my head against the tree. The rough bark pressed wavy lines into my skin. I was tired and soaked and sore and sad. Now would be as good a time as any to go home.

I lifted my head up. A large round light was floating right beside me. It was 'bout the same size as my goldfish bowl and shone bright yellow. I reached out to touch it but it zipped away from my fingertips. It stopped and hovered in the air. I raced towards it. My arms were bathed in its golden glow. I leapt up to catch it but it shot behind a tall pine tree. When I got to the other side of the tree it'd gone!

I spun round and round and round praying I'd see it again.

I peered ahead. Stars were shining in the sky. And stars were shining on the ground too. I could see two heavens! As I got closer, the stars on the ground rippled. That must be the pond the girl had been talking 'bout!

A small wooden bridge stretched over the twinkling

water to a cabin. It was just an ordinary plain old cabin, except for one thing: a giant tree grew out of its roof.

I could hear the wind chimes. They were hanging off the end of the bridge. Most wind chimes were made from wood or tin or glass or metal. This one was made from bones. My guts flipped the same way waffles do on a griddle.

That must be where Maymay lived! I'd be cuckoo to go home now after coming all this way. I crept over the bridge and tippy-toed up the cabin steps.

I reckoned it wouldn't do any harm peeking in through the window. It was dirty, so I wiped it with my sleeve. That was when I seen an old lady scowling right back at me.

11

I leapt back, knocking over a plant pot. It smashed into a million pieces.

The door opened and the woman appeared on the porch. Three bats flashed past her, straight into the cabin. "What is all this racket?" Her voice sounded as sharp as the broken pot shards on the floor. Her long dress was the same colour as a freshly dug grave, and she had a violet shawl draped over her shoulders. Whoever knitted it must have been real nervous 'cause it was full of holes.

"Well? Speak up!" she said.

My eyes found the steps. Two giant leaps and I could be in them woods.

She blinked at me like a crow. "What do you want?"

My mouth froze.

"Not the talkative type, are we? Fine by me. Don't let me catch you sneaking around my property again otherwise you'll regret it."

She turned to go back inside.

"A-are you Maymay?"

She muttered under her breath and turned to face me. "Who are you?"

"I have to speak to you."

"Come back another night – I'm busy."

There's no way I'd do that. Not after everything that'd happened tonight. It was now or never. "I brought you a special present," I said. "My name's Twister."

"You'd better come in then," she said, disappearing into the cabin.

I stood on the porch not right sure if I should follow her in or run away screaming.

She called out. "Hurry up before I change my mind."

As I stepped forward, my legs felt like they were made out of jelly. Jelly that ain't even set.

I smelled green leaves and liquorish and moths and bark and tobaccy and wax and orange peel and birds' nests. I swear there were more candles in here than at the church. Shadows twitched and swayed, all jittery.

Bang-slap in the middle of the cabin, a tree grew up through the floor and disappeared out a hole in the roof.

I'd never seen no tree on the *inside* before. Its lower branches were covered in Maymay's washing. I guess she wore raggedy vests too. Further up they were decorated with shoes and shells and torches and mirrors and dried flowers and wooden animals and stick people and feathers and stones. It looked as if the tree was laden with strange fruit.

I left the cabin door open, in case I needed to leave in a hurry.

"Were you born in a barn?" Maymay asked, glancing over at the door.

I gave her a look. "No – in a storm."

"Is that so," she said.

My heart sank some shutting it. With Point gone, I felt like a porcupine that'd lost its quills.

Maymay sat at a rickety table in front of a fire. She ought to slip a book under one of them legs to stop it from wobbling. Every time she moved, her bracelets tinkled. She sure wouldn't go surprising no bears in these woods.

The walls hid behind rows and rows and rows of shelves which were piggeldy-higgeldy and gleamed with jars.

"You're soaked through," she said. "Take something from the tree and change into it."

"I'm fine."

"You'll catch your death of cold. I can cure coughs and sniffles, but I can't perform miracles. Go and change."

I thought it best not to argue on this occasion. I grabbed a long blue shirt and crept behind the tree.

Some leaves rustled. A black hooty-owl with orange eyes gawped at me, its head bobbing up and down and up and down. Then it hissed at me. I put the shirt on and scooted out from behind the tree, throwing my clothes up on a branch to dry.

Maymay watched my every move without blinking. "Pull up a chair," she said.

I dragged one over, gently brushing off a spider clinging to the seat. Its skinny legs heaved its fat body off into the log pile for some quiet and peace.

Maymay's eyes were the colour of lily pads. One of

them had a black tear-shaped mark on it. How spooky! An always-crying eye. Her skin was thin and brown, like an ancient map you'd be scared to open in case it fallen to pieces.

I decided not to sit too close to her.

"What've you brought?" she asked.

I'd be mighty sorry to see the yellow kite go. I placed it on the table. Maymay examined the bit where the tail used to be.

"A bear cub took a fancy to it, but it'll still fly," I said.

She didn't say a word. My nerves jangle-jingled. "My dog chased after a ghost or something and never came back. Then I met a girl by Juniper Falls – she surprised me and I fallen into the pool but she happened to be friendly – she told me where to find you. I came face to face with a bear and one of her cubs ran off with the kite tail. I guess it could've been worse; the bear could've run off with my head or an arm or a leg. Aunt Honey told me you're a medicine woman and that you can speak to the dead…"

The look on her face shut me up. I picked at a scab on my elbow. I could hear them bones rattling outside in the wind. Maymay took a deep breath and something rattled inside her too. "Be grateful for all situations that come your way 'cause you learn from them," she said. "I don't take kindly to being called a medicine woman." She narrowed her eyes. "Nor am I a witch in case you were wondering. I prefer to think of myself as a caretaker of knowledge," she said. "I'll keep the kite."

She put a kettle on over the fire. And spooned some dried herbs into a teapot. "Hungry?" she asked.

I nodded. She popped some cookies on to a plate. "Pomple Root Crunches. Good for the soul if they don't break your teeth first."

The cookies were purple and the same shape as Merle and Gloria's poop. I hesitated. Pa had written in his letter that there was something I shouldn't take. That my life depended on it. What if Maymay had sprinkled poison in the cookie dough? I thought it best to wait until Maymay bit into one first. Her jaw clicked as she munched. Nothing happened – so I reckoned they must be safe after all. I chose the smallest one: it tasted of blackberries and caramel and oats and ginger beer and lettuce. After I'd finished chewing on it, I ran my tongue around my teeth to check they were all still there.

My eyes went exploring. They found a large skull

sitting on top of a pile of books. It grinned at me. I've seen rabbit skulls and crow skulls and lizard skulls and rat skulls and hog skulls and fish skulls and squirrel skulls and vole skulls and frog skulls and cow skulls. But I'd never seen no human skull before. A candle perched on top of its head and wax flowed like white blood into its eye socket.

"That was Mr Rouac. He suffered an adverse reaction to my Pomple Root Crunches," said Maymay.

I gasped. My hands flew up to my throat. I leapt to my feet, sending the chair clattering to the floor.

A flock of birds darted out from the tree and flapped around the cabin. Air whooshed out from Maymay's mouth. It had to be the strangest laugh I've ever heard.

The birds settled back in the tree.

"Mr Rouac's not real – he's made of clay. I've grown quite attached to him 'cause he never answers back."

I glared at her.

"Go on, sit down. It's clear you made your mind up 'bout me before we even met. It's far wiser to rely on your own intuition than to listen to the gossip of others," she said, lifting the plate of cookies up and offering them to me. "Perhaps you'd care for another?"

I shook my head. I'd had quite enough of Pomple Root Crunches for one day. And witches for that matter.

The kettle whistled. Maymay poured the hot water into the teapot and swirled it round and round and round, mumbling some words.

She sat down and filled the cups. As she stirred them, the spoon clanged softly. I loved that noise. It made me think of how Ma and Aunt Honey used to blether over tea and sugar biscuits at home. Home. It felt so very far away.

Maymay pushed a cup over to me. "This is Kickaburp Bliss tea. It's good for calming the nerves and encourages a balanced state of mind," she said, nodding at me to taste it.

Hot steam hit my face. I smelled pumpkin and sherbet drops and sunbeams and meadow grass and ladybirds and nettles and maple syrup. Again, I waited until Maymay had sipped hers first. She let out a loud burp which sounded much the same as the cry of a bullfrog. Aunt Honey would have considered that the height of bad manners.

I whole expected to hate the flavour of it. But I didn't. It fizzy-fuzzled on my tongue before sloshing down into my stomach. All of a sudden, my belly lurched. Before I could cover my mouth, I belched. The force of it made me spill my tea.

"The Kickaburp Bliss tea is relaxing you by releasing tension from the body. Here, have some more; you need it." Maymay topped up my cup. I settled back in my chair and carefully sipped at the tea.

Maymay lit a small pipe. Blue smoke snaked up towards the ceiling. She gazed at it as if she'd never seen it before. It didn't bother her three bits I couldn't stop burping.

"You seen many things in the woods tonight. It's good to be aware of everything around you; it could save your life one day," she said, puffing on her pipe.

A giant smoke ring wibbled above her head. I wanted to poke my finger through it. It widened and vanished.

Maymay cleared her throat. "You said your dog chased after a ghost. Ghosts exist but most people don't believe their eyes. Sadly, grown-ups have learned to see only what they wish to see."

I scratched my head. "Ghosts are real?"

"Everything gives off energy: you, me, trees, animals, birds, rocks, plants, rivers – everything. Ghosts do too, but they vibrate at a different frequency from us. Most people choose not to see them, but they can sense them all right."

She fished a hanky out of her sleeve and blew her nose. She tucked it away without even sneaking a peek to see what was in it. "You were frightened and lost your dog, but you still came to find me. This shows guts – either that or stupidity." Maymay smiled at me. "You trusted your instincts and talked to the girl. If you'd not spoken to her you might not have found me. Always trust your gut instinct – as I said before intuition ain't never wrong."

Maymay got up and emptied the remains of her pipe into the fire.

"You done well not to attack the bear. It's best never to use aggression when you feel fear. Bears want nothing to do with people, but they'd turn on you if they were starving or felt threatened. Luckily, the bear sensed you meant it no harm and that was why it left you alone. If someone slights you, you mustn't be tempted to seek revenge. If you do the only person you'll end up hurting is yourself. Only use force if your life depends on it."

A crease appeared on my brow.

"You're a deep thinker and you listen, which means

you've a true understanding of people. You're capable of so much more than you believe."

"That's nice of you to say," I said.

"I ain't here to be nice." She sipped her tea. "What do you want?"

"My pa's missing. I want to know what's happened to him. Can you help me?"

Maymay moved her teacup to one side. "You brought the kite. It's only fair I ask my spirit guides to see if they know anything."

"What's a spirit guide?"

"Someone who helps the living from the other side."

"Other side?" I asked.

"The spirit plane, you know, where the dead go."

My mouth felt dry. "You mean heaven?"

"Exactly, only better. If you've got something that belongs to your pa, we'll use it to try and find him," said Maymay. "But I warn you; the truth can hurt. If he's alive there's a possibility he might have lost himself to liquor, gambling or false promises."

"Pa ain't the sort."

"They never are," said Maymay.

I fetched my bag and rifled around inside it. I wasn't right sure if I had anything of his with me. I felt the coolness of the torch and reached further down. The blade of the penknife sliced my skin, making me yelp. I must have forgot to close it after getting scared by the deer. A thin line of red appeared on my finger. That was when I remembered it was Pa's.

I handed it to Maymay.

She lifted a bowl of tobaccy from the shelf. Maymay lit the brown leaves with a candle and fanned them. The colours around us faded as smoke filled the room. Maymay picked up the penknife and gripped it tight; her fingers were like bones that had been picked clean by the birds. She started to chant.

I could not believe my eyes.

Through the smoke, I seen every wrinkle on Maymay's face disappear. No amount of cold cream from Pearl Wiggle's salon could make her customers look this good.

The wind stirred and the cabin creaked. Jaggedy shadows snuck across the floor. The flames on the candles trembled.

Maymay muttered to herself real fast now.

The black hooty-owl screeched.

The cabin door blew open as if someone invisible had swept in to join us. The leaves in the tree and the candle flames all jumped.

I sprang up to shut the door. When I looked back, Maymay had slumped all rag-dolly over the table.

I rushed over to her. "Maymay. Maymay!"

She straightened up slowly.

"Are you OK?" I asked.

Maymay started choking. Her whole body jerked and twitched as black smoke shot out of her mouth and twisted high up into the air. For a split-moment it turned into the shape of a tall figure, then it whooshed out through the hole in the roof.

Aunt Honey said smoking stunted your growth. But she didn't tell me it made you cough up people-shaped clouds.

Maymay wheezed as if she'd been running up a mountain.

"Did your spirit guides see Pa?" I asked.

She squinted at me all funny. "He's trapped," she whispered.

"Trapped? Where?"

"It's dark."

"Is he alive?"

"It's not clear to me if he is on this plane or the spirit plane," she said.

"Can your guides go back and take another look?"

"No! They have spoken and must not be bothered again on the matter."

The top of my head tightened as a flash flood of anger washed through me. "I should never have come here! I lost my dog and my kite. And all for what?"

"We're done here. Go!" Maymay snarled. She pulled her shawl tight around her.

I stepped away. "I'm sorry. I didn't mean to upset you. It's just – you were my last hope. I thought you'd be the one person who could tell me for sure what'd happened to him. I miss him so much. And my ma's sick. If I could bring him home, she'd get better. I just know she would. I'd do *anything* to find him."

"Anything?"

"Cross my heart." I crossed my heart.

"And hope to die?" Her eyes glittered. "Perhaps I can help you. I'll give you a choice, so listen carefully. Accept your pa has gone and, if you leave now, I can guarantee you'll live a long life."

"What if I want him home?" I asked, quietly.

Maymay blinked. "There's a necklace that can help you."

"A necklace?"

Maymay glided over to the tree and yanked on a small branch. A door opened up in its trunk and Maymay ducked down and stepped through it. A few seconds later, there was a rumbling noise and then Maymay cussed from somewhere deep below.

The rumbling became ear-splitty.

Hundreds of bats spilled out from the trunk. Jars smashed and books tumbled and herbs scattered and spider webs snapped. I covered my head with my arms and hurried to the cabin door to fling it open. The bats brushed past me as they left.

Maymay reappeared holding a box. She didn't seem to notice the mess the bats had left behind. Stepping over broken glass, she placed the box in front of me. It was the same colour as storms.

"Take a look . . . go on," she urged.

I wiped my hands on my legs. She nodded her head. I undid the catch and lifted up the lid. Inside sat the most beautiful necklace I'd ever seen.

Maymay said, "The necklace is called Wah and there's something real important you should know 'bout it. It can lead you to your heart's desire but if you use it, you will be sure to die." I couldn't stop myself. I reached out to touch Wah. It felt warm as if someone had just taken it off. My fingers tangle-tingled. I swear I heard sighs all around me, though it must have been the wind in the trees.

The chain glowed fierce copper. Small shimmering discs hung off it. They tinkled sweetly when I picked it up. Not a noise you'd imagine warning you of danger.

The discs were covered in teeny-tiny etchings of animals and plants and insects and birds and water and fish and trees and people and mountains and clouds. They glittered and flashed, alive in the light.

In the middle of the necklace sat a round copper face with copper eyes and a copper nose and a copper mouth. It felt as smooth as church steps.

The necklace would lead me to my heart's desire.

The thought of having Pa back home again made my heart sing. Blood tore through my veins. I knew Wah held secrets. I felt drawn to it as a moth is to flame. I wanted nothing more than to put it on and feel it against my skin. But I stopped when I remembered Maymay's chilling words 'bout it leading to my death and all.

I placed Wah gentle as gentle could be back into its box. My fingers stopped tangle-tingling and my heart withered some. "It's 'bout the most wonderful thing I've ever seen, but it don't belong to me."

"Wah chooses its owner," said Maymay.

"Wah chooses its owner?"

"It's like having a parrot in here," she sighed.

"The necklace ain't yours?" I asked.

"Just 'cause I keep it out of harm's way don't mean it's mine," answered Maymay.

"What makes you think it has chosen me?"

"I asked my spirit guides who the owner would be. They sure had me stumped when they told me it'd be a twister, but my guides are never wrong. Happens I like twisters, they've great supernatural powers. You see, they represent the circle of life. When a twister arrives, it can

101

bring destruction and death but it leaves behind seeds and rainfall, which in turn creates new life."

"I think there's been some misunderstanding. I mean, I know I'm full of hot air and smash plant pots but I ain't a real twister."

"There's another reason I know it's yours."

I glanced back at Wah. Its smooth face twitched.

I gasped.

The necklace looked at me. Its copper mouth broke into the most enchanting smile I'd ever seen.

"Wah only ever comes to life for its true owner," said Maymay.

I couldn't tear my eyes away from it.

"I can see it ain't no ordinary necklace but how will it know where Pa is?" I asked.

Maymay sat herself down at the table. "Every time a man or an animal or a tree or a plant breathes out, a trace of their soul is left in the air. The wind blows in from the four corners of the globe, which means there's an awful lot of it floating around out there. The necklace can take this soul."

The bones rattled and clacked together outside.

I hadn't ever seen no souls in the air. If they really

were there you'd think you'd taste them, though I ain't right sure what they'd taste of. I reached out to stroke the necklace's face. It closed its eyes, same as Mew done when you petted her.

"Why would the necklace kill me?" I asked.

"Are you taking Wah?" asked Maymay.

I wanted to. Badly. But the words in Pa's letter came back to me. I knew for sure it was the necklace he had been warning me 'bout. That my life depended on this decision. I bit my lip. Ma's heart was already broken. If something happened to me it'd finish her off.

"I can't," I whispered.

"Then the matter of Wah endangering your life no longer concerns you." She snapped the lid on the box shut.

"I'd like to, Maymay. I just can't."

She appeared neither glad nor sad at my decision.

My shoulders slumped. A fog swirled around my head, my thoughts were scrambled. I lifted my head up to see Maymay's eyes burning bright.

"Your dog's safe," she said.

Something heavy lifted off my chest. "Point's OK? He's really OK?"

"He limps a little."

"Did Wah tell you this? Did you see his soul?"

"No, he's on the porch," Maymay replied, looking at me like I was as daft as a thrush.

"Point!" I ran out the door and threw myself at him. He wagged from the tip of his tail to the top of his nose. And licked my face, which was kinda yucky. But I let him seeing as how he wasn't dead and all. His coat was covered in leaves and mud and grass seeds and burrs.

When Point stopped his fussing, I seen the girl I'd met by Juniper Falls, standing on the porch.

"Found your dog catched up in some thorn bushes. He should get a medal for bravery 'cause there were fresh mountain lion prints in the mud. He must have been warning it off to protect you. The trees don't let the moonlight in there, so he can't have seen the bushes. He's got some nicks and scratches and I had to remove a thorn from his paw, but he's doing just fine."

"Did you say a mountain lion?"

"Told you there were all sorts in Holler Woods," she said, puffing her hair out of her eyes.

I scratched Point's neck. He closed his brown eyes, tilted his head to one side and opened his mouth. Point had most likely saved my life back there.

"Don't know what I'd do without him," I said. "I can't thank you enough for bringing him back to me."

"Oh, he found you. He's got a fine nose on him 'cause he tracked your scent all the way here. All I did was free him from the thorns. Your dog sure likes to pee. He pretty much lifted his leg on every trunk we passed on our way here."

I laughed and straightened up. "Say, what's your name?"

"I'm Beam," she said, waggling her head. "'Cause I'm always smiling."

"Pleased to meet you, Beam. I'm Twister," I said.

"What's all this commotion?" Maymay had come to the door.

"This is Beam," I said. "She found my dog, Point."

Beam's face shone. She clasped her hands behind her back and swayed from side to side.

Maymay stared at Beam. "I've had just 'bout enough excitement for one night. It's time you all left," she said. "Beam, think you could get this one back out of Holler Woods in one piece?"

"It'd be my pleasure, Maymay, seeing as how she's my friend and all," said Beam.

Maymay eyed Beam warily. "This is not a time for any of your mischief. You take her straight home or you'll have me to answer to."

Beam tutted and rolled her eyes.

"Glad that's settled then," said Maymay. "She'll be ready in a minute."

Point and me followed her back into the cabin. He refused to let me out of his sight for two seconds. Maymay handed me my clothes, which were dry and warm.

When I finished changing, I came out from behind the tree.

"We'll speak again," said Maymay.

Not if I could help it. But I kept that thought to myself.

"Next time, visit during the day," she said.

"You mean I didn't have to come here at night?"

Maymay's skin crinkled into a smile. "It's a measure of how much a person needs my help by what lengths they will go to, to see me."

Point raced around the cabin not sure whether to bark at the hooty-owl or snuffle at the spilled herbs or pee-pee against the tree.

"Bye, Maymay," I said.

Maymay crossed the floor silently to sit at her table.

"Mind that dog of yours," she said.

I closed the door real gentle behind me. And I was careful not to smash any plant pots on my way down the steps to where Beam was waiting for me.

What a night! I'd met a witch and found a magical necklace and discovered Pa was trapped somewhere and made a new friend. Whatever could happen next?

Ma's skin was white as unicorns, apart from the dark blue circles under her eyes. They matched her mood. We'd been picking strawberries for ages and she'd been as quiet as a graveyard. Before Pa left us, I had always known where she was on the farm. All I had to do was follow the sound of her laughter.

"At this rate, there'll be no strawberries left 'cause you'll have eaten them all," she scolded.

Strawberries were my most favourite food. Ever. Even the name said out loud was juicy and delicious. I loved picking them; I'd pop one in the basket and two into my mouth.

Point whined. He poked his nose through the fence and shifted his weight from one paw to another. I waited until Ma turned the other way and threw him one. He catched it and ate with his mouth open.

The wind blew strong, making Aunt Honey's undergarments wrestle with each other on the washing line.

I yawned. I liked yawning 'cause it felt good. Point shook his head when he yawned. That made his cheeks flap and he'd let out a squeak at the end of it. He was always real content afterwards too 'cause he'd stretch and wag his tail.

I'd yawned lots last night. Beam had walked us back through Holler Woods. She hadn't stopped talking the whole time. Happens that was a good thing as it meant I couldn't think 'bout what was lurking in the dark. Or dwell on the fact that I'd left the necklace behind. I was sure glad I'd met Beam. I hoped I'd see her again real soon.

"Ma? Once we've got enough strawberries, can I go fishing?"

"At Raging River?" she asked, pushing her hair out of her eyes with the back of her hand.

"Uh-huh."

"All right, you can go for an hour but don't you so much as dip a toe in the water," Ma said. "I don't care if you're a capable swimmer, the current's devilishly strong. And no quibbling either, otherwise you'll stay and help me make the jam."

"OK."

Ma's face softened. "Your pa loved fishing there too, not that he was any good at it. If he ever did catch something, he'd throw it back 'cause he didn't have the heart to end its life."

"I miss him, Ma." It escaped out of my mouth before I could stop it. I froze. I was under strict instruction from Aunt Honey not to go upsetting Ma.

Aunt Honey's bloomers cracked in the breeze. Proudfoot snorted in his field.

"Me too, Twist," she finally answered. Ma looked at me as if seeing me for the first time since he'd vanished. She paused and taken a big deep breath. "I pray every night he comes home. I imagine hearing the squeak of the gate and me rushing out of the house. And there he is, standing, right in front of me. He's had the fight of his life returning to us, but it's him all right." Ma patted her hair and smoothed down her top. Her smile faded as she slowly came back to the strawberry patch. "Honey is convinced he'll show up, but the more time passes, I ain't so sure." Ma looked so frail I was scared she'd tumble away in the wind. "I wish I didn't love him so darn much," she whispered.

My heart ached. Every beat pushed the hurt around my body. I thought 'bout the letter hidden in my room and I thought 'bout Maymay telling me Pa was trapped. I felt ashamed I'd turned down the chance to find him. My cheeks flushed apple red with the guilt. Had I made the wrong decision 'bout Wah?

Ma wearily brushed the soil and straw off her legs. I seen her trying her best to sweep away all her sad thoughts too. "Think we've earned ourselves a break."

Aunt Honey appeared, walk-running along the side of the barn. She raced past us. "No time to stop and gossip with you ladies," she panted. "I've a call of the wild to attend to." Aunt Honey got different names for when she needed to go. If it was an emergency, a call of nature turned into a call of the wild.

Point torn round the side of the fence to chase

after her. He barked and Aunt Honey shrieked and the chickens flapped. I swear it snowed feathers.

I sat at my favourite spot, next to the crooked maple tree. The tree don't have any leaves on it, but it wore a fine coat of ivy to stop it from blushing. I gazed out across Raging River. The water was light blue by the bank and dark blue further out and white and frothy under the bridge 'cause the rocks made it so.

Point sniffed at the vole burrows by the water's edge. A dragonfly buzzed on over to him, making him flap his ears. He climbed back up the bank and threw himself into some long grass, letting out a big sigh. I guess he was pretty tired after last night's adventures in Holler Woods too.

Something tugged at my line. I started to reel it in.

"Hey, Twistie. Wotcha up to?"

I nearly let go of the fishing rod. Beam sure was good at appearing when I least expected it.

"Catched myself a fish, want to see?" I said.

"Sure!" She plonked herself down in the shade. Her white dress billowed around her. It still had mud on it.

I gritted my teeth, as I pulled with all my might.

"Think you might be the first person in Culleroy to hook a whale in Raging River," she said.

"Whatever it is feels bigger than a whale," I gasped.

I tugged and tugged and tugged on the line. Beam held her breath. Just as I thought the line would snap, the hook shot out of the water. Except there wasn't a fish on the end of it. Or a whale. Only an enormous clump of river weed.

"Congratulations, Twistie! You catched yourself a green fish," said Beam, slapping her knees with her hands.

"Very funny," I said, wiping sweat off my brow with my sleeve. I removed the slimy weeds and tossed them back into the river, then placed the rod down beside me. As soon as I done that, I spied some trout leaping around in the river.

"I ain't seen a girl fishing here before," said Beam.

"You might not see one again if I hook any more weeds. Looks like I've got my pa's gift for scaring the fish away."

"Forgot to ask – does Maymay know where he is?" Beam tilted her head. She had three moles on her cheek, all sat in a row. I've seen the same pattern of stars in the night sky. When she talked, her nostrils flared. I liked how they done that. Even though Beam and I had not long met, I trusted her.

"Maymay thinks he's trapped somewhere, but she don't know where for sure. She has a necklace that might be able to find him though." I glanced at Beam. Whole expecting she'd poke fun at me for telling her a piece of jewellery could do something that Sherriff Buckstaffy and the folks of Culleroy couldn't.

"That's great she can help you!" she said.

I swatted a buzzy-fly away from my face. "You think a necklace really could find him?"

"I think if you believe in magic, it happens," she said, shrugging.

I swallowed. "Thing is, if I use this necklace, Maymay says there's a catch."

"A catch?"

"There'll be a catch as in something would happen to me."

"Like what?"

"I'd lose my life. Or something like that."

The smile slipped from Beam's face. She leapt to her feet. "Twistie! Magic or no magic, *nothing* is worth dying over."

"It's tearing me apart knowing he's trapped somewhere. And you should have seen my ma today. I've not just lost Pa – I'm losing her too!"

Beam stamped her foot. "Your ma will never recover if anything happens to you. Nor would your pa ever want you to risk your life for him, trapped or not trapped. And you know that's true. It would be selfish of you to take that necklace – your family needs you here. And how do you even know you can trust Maymay?" she yelled.

My mouth fallen open.

I'd never known someone full of so much joy could be full of so much anger too. I kicked at a clump of grass.

I hated to admit it but she was right. It'd finish Ma off if I got myself killed. And Pa would never want me risking my life for him. He had warned me 'bout Maymay in his letter. Perhaps taking Wah was a terrible idea after all.

"Well?" said Beam. "What are you going to do?"

"Not take it. Satisfied?"

"Really?"

"It's probably for the best," I muttered.

Beam sat herself down next to me. "You sure had me going there for a minute."

I counted the spots on a ladybug as it crawled across my foot.

Beam gave me a nudge. I nearly fallen over with the force of it.

"We still friends?" she asked.

"If you quit trying to push me over."

Beam smiled again and started to pick daisies.

"You hungry?" I asked. "Aunt Honey's making pancakes for tea. You'd be more than welcome to join us. We could get that dress of yours washed too, so it's as good as new."

"No!" said Beam. "I mean, no thank you. I've got stuff to do. I'd best be going."

"Some other time perhaps?"

Beam yawned and stretched. Point snuffled around in a patch of tall, every-colour flowers by the bank. He popped out covered in yellow dust and sneezed seven times. An orange flower landed on his ear.

"Why, Point! I reckon you could win a rosette for being Best In Show." Point raced over and tucked his head under my arm. I scratched his neck. He closed his brown eyes, tilted his head to one side and opened his mouth.

Beam laughed.

"Beam?"

"Yup?"

"Why'd you get so mad when I told you 'bout the necklace?"

She stood with her hands on her hips. "Life is precious, Twistie. Besides I've only just found you. Can't bear the thought of losing you is all." With that, she twirled on her heels and disappeared off down the path. She raised her hand and waved without so much of a backwards glance in our direction. And in that very moment, I knew for sure Beam was the bestest friend I'd ever had.

Aunt Honey yelled at me to hurry up. I popped the snickerbugs into a jam jar and put them into my bag where it would be nice and dark. I took my time going down the stairs, careful not to bump them.

"A snail could beat you to school. Wipe that jam off your mouth otherwise Miss Ida will think there's a clown attending her class," said Aunt Honey. She'd baked fresh scones for breakfast. They were heaven on a plate with melty butter and Ma's strawberry jam.

Aunt Honey tapped my head. "You brushed your hair?"

"Uh-huh."

"And I'm Bozo the Great Magician. Now skedaddle! And no dilly-dallying to gawp at the wildlife."

Point and me flew out the door. The clouds must be sad today 'cause they were the colour of cement and scraped across the tops of the trees.

I ordered Point to stay at the gate, but he woofed. I guess me and Pa and Ma and Aunt Honey weren't the only stubborn ones in the family.

We hurried along the path and over the bridge.

A breeze shook the trees awake. The black rooster on the barn roof had twirled in every direction, which meant the wind blew in from all four corners of the world. I thought 'bout what Maymay had told me. If there really were souls floating around, the air must be full of them.

I stuck my tongue out to see if I could taste anything. But I couldn't.

Everything felt lighter inside me today. I'd Beam to thank for making me see sense 'bout Wah. I just had to believe that Pa would come home when he could. And until then, I'd do my best to make Ma happy again in the hope that it would make her feel better.

Miss Ida rang the bell. The wind made it sound as if the school was a million miles away. She sure would be pleased I'd brought the snickerbugs. After class, I'd go to Cedar Creek Lake and release them 'cause they'd be missing their friends.

Point halted and snuffled the air. He stiffened. Had he smelled the souls? I marched forward to see what was bothering him. A figure stepped out from the bushes.

I'd been so busy thinking 'bout Pa and Ma and Beam, I plain forgot to worry 'bout Clem Hussable. He stood there, all snot and scabs and greasy hair.

"Fancy seeing you here," he said, in a way that said he wasn't the least bit surprised to see me.

Point flattened his ears and tucked himself in at my legs. Clem lunged and snatched the bag off my shoulder. He'd a grubby bandage on his finger where I'd bit him. And a cut on his cheek. But I was certain I never done that.

He opened my bag and found the sandwiches and an apple. He stuffed the sandwiches into his pockets and bit into my apple. He wrinkled his nose up and tossed it away.

I glanced around to see if anyone was coming, but

we were alone except for the crow in the tree above us. It chose to look the other way.

Clem stuck his hand back into my bag.

"What do we have here?" he said, bringing the jar of snickerbugs out and holding it up to the light. "See you brought some friends with you." His teeth were like the crooked stones in the churchyard.

"Give them here, Clem," I spat.

"Or what, Twister? You'll bite me again?" His eyes became smaller and meaner. "Or maybe you'll set your pa on me?"

My guts tightened. Point whined and twisted but I held him close.

"Keep that fleabag away or else." Clem unscrewed the lid of the jar. "Miss Ida asked you to bring these in for class today, didn't she? You're quite the golden girl."

He took the lid off and shook it. The snickerbugs spread their church-window wings and flew off to find some shade.

"Whoops," he said. "Guess Miss Ida won't be too happy with you now." He hurled the jar away. It smashed. Point whined.

"I'll be waiting for you later." Clem kicked my bag so

hard it flew into the bushes. He sprinted off towards the school.

My heart hurt with beating so fast. Point nudged my leg with his nose. I patted his head and fetched my bag from the bushes. "Go home! Go on. Away with you!" I made my voice all low and cutty-sharp. He needed to understand it wasn't ever safe with Clem 'bout.

I walked away from him. When I reached the schoolyard, I stopped to check if Point had gone. He was still on the path, watching my every move.

The class had already started when I burst through the door. The scowling boys and prissy girls held their breaths to see if I'd get into trouble, but Miss Ida only told me to settle myself.

"Did you remember to bring the snickerbugs, Twister?" she asked.

I flicked my eyes at Clem. He smirked. If I grassed him up, there was no telling what he might do to me after school.

"No, Miss Ida," I said. "I'm sorry. I forgot."

She peered down her glasses at me and pursed her lips. "First you're late and now you've not done the one thing I specifically asked you to do. Extra arithmetic for you every night this week and you can stay behind after class to clean the board. Everyone, open your books at page forty-seven."

"Think you can do that, Twister? Clean the board? You're so dumb I doubt you could even get that right," hissed Cherry.

The other girls smiled but their eyes glittered cold. I ain't sure what I'd done to make them hate me so much. I thought of Beam and the sunshine in her voice and wished she was here.

The day dragged on and on and on. Worse still, I felt Clem staring at me the whole time. When Miss Ida eventually dismissed the class, him and the boys scarpered out the door.

As I rubbed the chalk numbers off the blackboard, I catched sight of them skulking amongst the trees.

The way I seen it I'd two choices: I could make a run for it or get the fight over and done with. Clem had to punish me for biting him. If I dodged him today, he'd just come after me tomorrow, or the day after that. He'd keep on coming for me until he'd taught me a lesson in front of his boys.

I wiped my chalky hands on the back of my shorts. I'd made my mind up.

I walked out the door and crossed the schoolyard and strode right on over to them.

Surprise filled their eyes. Even the wind stilled to see what would happen. Clem swept his lank hair out of his dead eyes with a filthy hand.

"Well, well. If it ain't little Miss Perfect. What you doing here? Looking for more snickerbugs?" The boys yipped.

"I'd much rather be in a snickerbug's company than yours – they're way more interesting," I said.

"There you go again with that mouth of yours. It's always getting you in trouble. I think it's time I shut you up." He glanced at the boys. "Hey, how do you get a twister to twist?" he asked. They grinned at each other 'cause they knew they were in for a treat.

Clem stamped on my foot. Hard. Bones crunched. I fallen to the ground, writhing in agony.

The boys formed a circle around us. No escaping now.

A foot kicked my spine. A mouth spat. A hand yanked my hair. My pain excited them.

I burned. My insides boiled so hot, the hurt vanished.

I scrambled on to my feet. Clem's mud-brown eyes wavered for a split-moment. His dirty mouth opened as I raised my fist. I punched him with every bit of strength I had.

His nose squished under my knuckles. Clem dropped to his knees, his snot flowing red.

A man burst into the circle and grabbed Clem by the scruff of the neck. He hauled him up. Clem's watery eyes widened when he seen who it was.

I guess the sun hadn't been too welcome in prison. The red scar on his neck and the naked blue lady on his arm were the most colourful things 'bout Hack Hussable. I ain't clapped eyes on him for a long time, but it was him all right. It was a wonder they had kept Clem's pa inside for so long 'cause he was as skinny as spider silk. You'd think he'd have been able to slip right on out through the bars.

Hack let go of Clem. His eyes were the colour of axe blades. Clem wiped the blood from his nose.

"What you staring at?" growled Hack. The boys lost their grins. They snatched their bags and melted away into the trees.

"You stupid boy," said Hack. His tongue wet his lips. "Getting hit by a girl? Do you want them to think you're weak?" His yellow fingers stroked the stubble on his chin.

I smelled his breath. All stale liquor and damp walls and sticky tar. "I'm gonna have to toughen you up. Huh?" Hack cuffed Clem on the chin. "Huh?" He done it again. Clem's skin reddened.

"You got something for me?" Hack asked.

Clem stood still as icicles. Hack swore under his breath. "He's so slow you'd be mistaken for thinking he'd been dropped on his head as a baba."

Life returned to Clem. His hands flew into his pockets and he pulled out two coins and a marble and some bubblegum.

"How am I supposed to quench my thirst with this?" Hack turned and scowled at me. "What's your name?"

"Twister," I whispered.

Hack's eyes were blank. And then they flickered.

"You're the girl whose pa went missing?"

My knees knocked together.

"He was quite the talk of the jail, I can tell you. We even placed bets on it. Most of them thought he'd a score to settle with Turrety Knocks and that's why he started the fire. But it always struck me your pa was the gutless type. He didn't have what it takes to kill a man, never mind a woman and child. So, I put my money on him running off with a fancy lady. Smart move as it happens with no wife to nag him and no kid to disappoint him. I might be tempted to disappear with a fancy lady myself." His laugh sounded much the same as steam being released from a valve. "I guess we'll find out in good time what he really got up to."

Hack crouched down and shoved his hand into my bag. I kinda regretted that I'd stuffed thorny branches into it at lunchtime. I'd wanted to make Clem think twice 'bout stealing from me again. Hack yanked his hand back out. There were white lines and beads of blood on the back of it.

"Right little firecracker, ain't you?" he said, leaning forward and taking a handful of my hair. He pulled me in close.

"You may be sharper than my boy; lord knows, it wouldn't take much, but you showed him up in front of his friends. And do you know what's going to happen? Clem's going to go home in a mood and this'll make Mrs Hussable cranky. And when she gets cranky, it's *yak*, *yak*, *yak* in my ear, which makes me real mad. A thinking man such as myself needs his peace and quiet – now don't look so alarmed, Twister, this here's a friendly conversation.

Strike my boy again and you and me will be having another one of these chats. Except it won't be quite so civil the next time around." He licked his cracked lips and his tongue slip-slided back into his dark mouth.

I stopped breathing so I wouldn't have to smell him no more. I stared at Clem. He glared back at me.

"It's been a real pleasure meeting you. You be sure to pass on my regards to your ma." Hack let go of me and slapped me on the backside.

I picked up my bag and ran. The trees and flowers and plants and bushes turned into an ugly green and brown smudge.

Point sat waiting for me at the gate. He rushed forward to greet me. I hugged him and buried my face into his fur, until Hack's bad smells were chased away by Point's sweet scent.

"There you are! You're late. Supper's nearly ready," said Aunt Honey. Her cheeks were hot-stove pink. "Twist, look at the state of you. You'd be forgiven for thinking you've spent the entire afternoon hog-wrestling."

The kitchen smelled of fish oil and parsley and butter and strawberries and warm sugar.

"Are you limping?" she asked.

"I hurt my foot."

"Want me to take a look at it?"

"Nope."

"I've never known anyone so eager to have an accident. Except for your Great-Uncle Cee: he could've knocked himself unconscious in a room full of feathers."

Three pieces of trout sizzled in the pan. Mew pretended to snooze on top of the cupboard.

I sat at the table. Point lay by my feet, ready to pounce if a morsel of food dropped off my fork.

Aunt Honey slapped the fried fish on to plates and brought them over to the table. "Get tore in, it's just the two of us tonight."

"Is Ma OK?" I asked.

"She's flat out 'cause she made another fifty pots of jam this afternoon. There are not just strawberries, sugar and pectin in them jars. Your ma's heart and soul are in there too."

Aunt Honey sniffed her food like it was a bunch of flowers. She spun the plate round and grabbed her fork and knife.

The trout tasted sweet and salty and earthy and

delicious. I dolloped some buttery mash on to my plate.

"Have some carrots, Twist, they'll help you see in the dark," said Aunt Honey.

I wasn't so sure I wanted my eyes glowing like torch beams, but I took a couple of them anyways.

"I called in at Turrety Knocks's today. Did I not find the old coot full of beans? He reckons he's done with the drink, and I think he really means it this time. I handed over some food supplies. He was mighty pleased and gave me the fish, which he'd reeled in this morning with his very own fair shaking hands. I hope he starts taking better care of himself, there's a fine man hiding under all that grief." Aunt Honey sipped some water from her glass. She gently dabbed the corners of her mouth with a napkin and attacked the fish with the ferocity of a starving bear.

"Maybe you could make him happy again, Aunt Honey?"

Aunt Honey gasped. "Twist, what are you trying to imply?"

The thought of her strolling around holding hands with Turrety Knocks made me snort.

"What's so funny?" she asked. "I used to be considered

quite a catch back in the day. My name's been carved more than the one time on that giant oak in Holler Woods." Aunt Honey winked at me.

"Someone scratched *White Eye will get you* on the same tree."

"I've courted a few unsavoury types in my time but I never stooped that low." On hearing Aunt Honey's laughter, Point scooted out from underneath the table. He wagged his tail, hoping for a tasty titbit of fish. Aunt Honey ignored his pleading eyes. "I swear, if you so much as missed one of his feeds, you'd be in grave danger of being eaten alive," she huffed.

"Where did that tale 'bout White Eye come from anyway?"

"Part of Culleroy folklore, I guess. The story goes there was an old medicine man who used his powers to do bad things. When one of the village elders' daughters went missing, he was driven out by the locals, which led to his death. And far from resting in peace, he reaped his revenge by killing people and stealing their souls."

"Do you believe it?"

"It's a load of old hokey. But parents are mighty thankful 'cause the threat of White Eye coming has seen generations of children off to their beds on time, without so much of a peep out of them."

"Clem Hussable sure believes in White Eye."

"Hack Hussable's son?" asked Aunt Honey.

"Uh-huh."

"I'm sure Hack will have scared his boy witless with the story."

"Hack Hussable was at the school today."

"He was? They must have released him from Gravelswitch Jail. The man's nothing but a tick in the grass, waving his arms around to see who he can latch on to and bleed dry next. He'll be here asking us for work before you know it, but he don't know the meaning of the word. What's that Clem like?"

"He ain't no good neither," I said.

"Hack's always been handy with his fists, especially with a drink in him. I dare say Clem's been bearing the brunt of his temper for years. Stay away from them both, they're trouble."

"I will."

Aunt Honey nodded. "Once you've finished, could you check on the animals while I take Ma her supper? There are scraps for the hogs in the bucket."

"Uh-huh."

"We can have a hot chocolate by the fire later."

Aunt Honey's hot chocolate sure would be a pleasant ending to what'd been an awful day.

Outside, deep pinks and purples and blues nudged against each other in the sky. The stars were getting ready for their evening performance. One of the chickens squawked. Point sniffed the air and tore off towards the barn. He knew there'd be a hen hiding in there.

The rest of the chickens were gulping in the yard. I rounded them up into the coop, where Gorgeous George strutted around. Some of the hens near swooned in his presence. His red and orange feathers sure were colourful. Sometimes they gleamed so bright in the sunshine it was as if he was on fire.

Point barked ferocious in the barn. I went to see what all the fuss was 'bout. As I walked in, a head ducked down behind the straw bales. Point stamped his front feet and growled. Chicken-bumps appeared on my arms.

"Who's there?" I said. A hen squawked and straw rustled. "If you don't show yourself, I'll yell and folks will come running."

Someone moved in the shadows. They held a chicken by its feet. It stopped flapping and decided to play dead.

"That ain't yours. Give it here."

"I ain't taking no orders from a girl." Clem Hussable stepped into the light. One of his eyes was purple swollen. He gripped the cold, rusty knife in his hand.

My heart beat loudly in my ears. "Get out of here, Clem."

"You made a fool of me in front of my pa." His voice trembled. He took another step towards me.

"You managed to do that all by yourself," I said. "Point, come here!" Point stayed rooted to the spot. "Point!" He crept silent as a ghost over to my side. I held on to him.

Clem's face shone with sweat. "I ain't ever seen him as mad as he was tonight," he said.

I glanced around the barn. A rake and a pitchfork were hanging up on the wall.

He came closer. The hen sprang back to life. It squawked and flapped, giving me a fright. It startled Clem too. He tossed it away. The chicken picked itself up and fled behind a straw bale.

"If you leave now, I'll forget you were ever here, Clem."

He wiped his face with a grimy sleeve. "It's all right for you; you don't have a pa to knock you around." Clem moved forward. "And look at you living on a big old farm. You're nothing but a spoilt brat."

"I'm sorry 'bout your pa," I said. "Really I am. I shouldn't have hit you. And I'm real sorry he don't care 'bout you neither."

Every muscle in Clem's body tensed. "Pa *does* care 'bout me. Why! There you go again with that lying mouth of yours. I should've cut your tongue out when I'd the chance." He leapt at me. One of his hands gripped my throat, stealing my voice. I looked into his eyes. There was no life in them.

I staggered back, letting go of Point, who snarled wild and launched himself at Clem. He shrieked and released me. Clem turned and lashed out at Point with his boot, but Point jumped out of the way just in time.

I seen my opportunity; the barn door was open. I could fetch help. I started to run.

Point made a strange, high-pitched noise.

I skidded to a halt and whirled round.

Point lay on the ground with the rusty knife sticking out of his chest. The golden straw beneath him grew dark.

"Next time, it'll be you, Twister," gasped Clem. He trip-stumbled out of the barn into the night.

"Point!" I wailed, dropping to his side. He licked my hand, but his tail wasn't wagging. He panted fast as if he couldn't breathe proper.

My eyes dripped. I cradled his head and whispered into his black ears. "Please don't go, Point. Please. We'll chase the rabbits on Black Smoke Hill tomorrow. And I'll find us another kite to fly – you can catch the tail next time. I promise."

Point closed his brown eyes, tilted his head to one side and opened his mouth. Except this time, I wasn't scratching him on his favourite spot.

Clouds covered up the sky 'cause blue was way too bright and happy a colour to see today. And the trees had nothing to say. They drooped their branches instead.

Turrety Knocks stood with his hat off. His eyes were red. But they were mostly always like that. He sniffed. Ma swayed. She reached out to Aunt Honey to steady herself. The climb to the top of the field had taken it out of her.

I looked down into the hole in the ground. Point lay there. Sleeping. Bye-bye, Point. Wrapped up in his favourite green tartan blanket.

A lump rose in my throat and my eyes stung.

"It's time to put his things in with him," Aunt Honey said, softly.

I knelt and placed his red squeaky ball and his go-fetchy stick and all different kinds of paper beside him. I slipped in some shooglepopple candy too. Even Point loved shooglepopple candy.

"Do you want to say something, Twist?" Aunt Honey asked.

I stood up. I tried to speak but my throat was way too tight. No words would come out.

Aunt Honey stepped forward. "We're here to thank Point for giving us much joy and happiness in our lives. I'll never forget the uproar he caused when he stole Posey Flannigan's underwear from her washing line. Happens he done her a favour 'cause the lace would've been far too itchy for that giant behind of hers anyway."

Ma gave Aunt Honey a dig in the ribs with her elbow. Aunt Honey sighed and her words slowed. "I know I was always cussing him. He'd chase the chickens, hide my socks, pee in the vegetable patch and get under my feet at every opportunity he could in the kitchen. I was woken most days by the squeak of his ball. That was his way of telling me it was time for his breakfast." Aunt Honey's voice cracked like mud in the sun.

Turrety Knocks shifted in his boots.

Aunt Honey paused to clear her throat. "As it happens, the thing that drove me mad 'bout him was the thing I loved best 'bout him – his spirit. And he showed this spirit right up until the very end. We'll miss him terribly. Point will forever be in our hearts." Aunt Honey's face shone with tears. Turrety Knocks brought out his hanky and handed it to her. She blew her nose.

I felt a cool hand slip into my mine. I didn't even have to look to see who it was. Beam squeezed my fingers.

Ma dabbed her eyes with a tissue. Turrety Knocks picked up the shovel and started to fill the grave in. The green tartan blanket turned brown. When he finished, he patted the earth down with the back of the shovel.

"Turrety Knocks: we can't thank you enough. You'll come to the house for some tea and cake?" asked Aunt Honey.

"No need for thanks," he muttered, shuffling over to us.

"Point was a fine dog, Twister," he said. He leant in and whispered, "If Clem comes near you again, you let me know." For a split-moment his faded moss and bark eyes glittered fierce. He tipped his hat at Beam and me.

Aunt Honey called over. "Don't stay out too long," she said. "You're welcome to invite friends back to the house, if you want." She smiled a sad smile at us.

Turrety Knocks hooked his arm under Ma's. Aunt Honey took her other arm and they set off down the field.

"Can't tell you how sorry I am 'bout Point, Twistie," said Beam.

We went to sit under the apple tree. This was Point's favourite spot. He'd half close his eyes in the sun with his shiny nose twitching. From here he could see the whole farm; he'd watch the chickens pecking and the hogs scratching and Merle and Gloria grazing and Proudfoot swishing his tail.

The grey clouds dragged themselves across the sky.

"Wanna do something?" Beam asked.

"Think I'll take a walk."

"We could go to Juniper Falls and catch some green fish?"

"I wouldn't be much company."

Beam tore at the grass with her hands. "I wish I could make all this go away."

I knew exactly how she felt. Every time I closed my eyes, I seen Clem's face and the cold, rusty knife. If I'd cried out for help or sent Point out of the barn, he'd still be here. It was my fault he'd died. I never should have punched Clem. Maymay had been right 'bout one thing; if you hurt someone, it ends up hurting you way more.

Aunt Honey went crazy-cuckoo when she discovered us in the barn. She'd wanted to drive straight round Clem's house to confront him. But with Hack out of jail, Ma warned her it'd be way too dangerous.

Ma thought we ought to tell Sheriff Buckstaffy. Aunt Honey said he'd just give Clem a slap on the wrist for trying to steal a chicken and killing a dog. Dogs didn't count for much around these parts. Neither of them had a clue Clem had threatened to kill me.

Aunt Honey called in on Miss Ida. She told her I wouldn't be coming back to school with Clem still there. Miss Ida promised she'd expel Clem if she ever catched him with a knife. She handed over a whole load of books, so I could continue my studies at home.

Beam rested her head against the tree. "Point loved you so much, Twistie. You seen it in his eyes every time he looked at you." She stretched out and patted my hand.

"Thanks for being here," I said. "But you should go and put a vest on 'cause you're freezing."

"Won't your ma be worried if you go for a walk alone?" she asked.

"Ma always frets 'bout me. But if she thinks it'll make me less unhappy today, she won't say nothing."

Beam studied my face. "Wherever you're off to, you be careful."

I got up and strode towards the trees. A rabbit jumped through the fence at the bottom of the field. It ran as fast as its legs could carry it and threw itself into its burrow. I wondered if that had been Point chasing it. Boy, how he'd loved chasing the rabbits.

Maymay don't look so scary in the daylight. I found her drinking tea on her porch steps. Funny thing was, she'd already poured out two cups. She handed me one and I sniffed it. It wasn't Kickaburp Bliss tea. This one smelled of still-on-the-tree apples and warm biscuits and rosehip and pear and pink grapefruit and fresh dew. I took a sip and I didn't belch, not once.

My heart weighed heavy. I'd had to drag it the whole way here. I missed Point so much I wanted to scream. But

I was frightened if I did, it would be so loud the ground would shake and trees would flatten and the sky would come crashing down.

Walking wasn't the same without Point. It was as if a part of me was missing: I was off balance. And the silence hurt my ears. I'd never felt so alone. There was no woofing or tail thumping or splish-splashing or sniffing or digging or sneezing or panting or whining or yawning or huffing or puffing.

I felt light. Like air flowed through my veins instead of blood. A breeze brushed over my skin. It tickled. Maymay's voice sounded far away.

"Silver Cloudtip tea lifts the spirits. If you've never had it before, I suggest you hold on to something immediately."

I was no longer on the steps. I'd floated up to the tree that grew out of Maymay's roof! A jade hopper bird dropped four wiggling worms when I drifted past. Maymay yelled at me to come back. I grabbed a branch and pulled myself on to the roof. Then I clung leech-strong on to the ivy and worked my way down the front of the cabin, landing softly on the porch.

"It's rude floating off when someone's trying to talk

to you. Here, take this." Maymay passed me a large stone. I placed it on my lap so I wouldn't act like a lost balloon at the fair again.

"I can't bring your dog back," she said.

I stared at her. Aunt Honey always said bad news travelled faster than shooting stars in Culleroy. I picked at some dried drops of candlewax on the step. The wax wedged itself under my fingernail.

"He's passed over to the spirit plane," she said, taking a big sip of her tea. "But he returns to give the rabbits a hard time."

This should have made me happy. But I suddenly felt his loss all the more. He should be here, with me. Hot tears made dark splotches on my shorts.

"You're quiet for a twister," said Maymay. Her eyes were a different colour in the sun, more of a grape-green than a lily pad-green. But the tear mark was still as black as a bear's nose.

Ma's health worsening and Point forever gone and Clem threatening to finish me off sure made the decision 'bout the necklace real easy. "Ma needs Pa back home more than ever. I do too. I'll do whatever it takes," I said, sniffing loudly.

Maymay tilted her head, reminding me of a crow figuring out how to prise a snail from its shell.

"The necklace itself won't harm you. However, if you seek its help a man by the name of White Eye will come for you. It'll be him who'll try to end your life."

"White Eye?" I said.

"White Eye."

"I ain't a kid, Maymay," I said. "I know he ain't real."

Maymay kept her voice low and steady. "I'll tell you what he did that was clever: he made people around here believe he didn't exist, that he was just an old story. And when he killed to steal souls, nobody thought he could have done it 'cause he wasn't real, which meant White Eye got away with murder."

I shifted uncomfortably on the step and the stone moved on my lap. Its coldness seeped into my skin.

"White Eye's as real as you or the trees or that cup you're drinking from." Maymay turned to me. "I understand this is difficult to take in. It would be easier to continue believing he was a character from a tale, but this would put you in grave danger. All I ask is that you stay open to the possibility he walks amongst us; it could help save your life."

Something in the tone of her voice made me think it wise to pay attention to her. "OK, I'm listening," I said.

"White Eye was one of the first to settle in Culleroy over two hundred years ago."

"He's two hundred years old?"

"Correct."

"Are you the same age?"

Maymay narrowed her eyes at me. "White Eye is also a keeper of knowledge. In the world of magic, you can open the door to light and goodness, or you can open it to darkness. Being good all the time is a pain in the backside 'cause it's much harder work, so he chose to embrace the darkness."

"Do you?" I asked.

"Almost never," said Maymay. She continued on. "When he arrived, there wasn't a town or a church or shops – but there was fertile land to grow crops on, woods to shelter in and a river to drink from. It didn't take long before folks flocked here from far and wide. He hated this and moved deeper into the woods to avoid them. One by one, the locals started to fall ill. They turned to another keeper of knowledge who lived on Misty Peaks. Her name was Wah."

"The necklace is named after her?" I said.

Maymay nodded. "She told them White Eye had poisoned the water to drive them away. Not long after the village elder's daughter went missing. Everyone was certain White Eye was responsible. They tracked him to a cave he lived in; the floor was littered with bones and the air filled with the stench of death. The villagers never found the girl's bright blue cape nor her body, but certain of his guilt, they chased him out of Culleroy, straight into the path of an ice storm. They knew full well he couldn't survive it. Over the noise of the howling wind, White Eye cursed them. He told them he'd come back and take the lives of their children."

"So, the story is true 'bout him," I whispered.

"Never in their wildest dreams did the villagers think White Eye would cheat death. He learned that if he killed and stole the souls of others, he could live. If you can call it living, as he is neither alive nor dead. Undead would be a more accurate description."

I was not right sure what she meant by that. But I didn't say nothing 'cause I wanted her to carry on.

"People started reporting sightings of White Eye to the village elders and doubt crept into their minds. They once again consulted with Wah and she made a necklace for them that turned cold when White Eye was near, so they could always hide the children from him. And if he approached the villagers, Wah could take souls from the air so they could protect themselves against his sorcery." Maymay sat silent for a while. I let her words sink in. A shiny green shieldy bug landed on her violet shawl. She neither noticed nor cared.

"Why do people not believe he is real any more?"

"White Eye left Culleroy to travel far and wide, so the sightings of him stopped. The villagers convinced themselves that he really had died. As the years passed, their fear faded and he became a tale to be told around fires at night. Even the necklace became nothing more than a local legend."

"But you think he's back?"

"He has been for a while."

The thought of him sneaking around gave me the creeps. "Why is he here?"

"Nothing lasts for ever, Twister. White Eye's body is old and starting to fail him," she said. "The dead souls he's taking ain't working as good as they used to. In time, he will crumble into dust and cease to exist."

"Ain't that a good thing?" I asked.

"It has made him all the more determined to find Wah while he can."

Even though it was sticky in the heat, I shivered. I peered into the black gaps between the trees, half expecting to see a face staring back at me.

"Why does he want the necklace so bad?"

"Wah takes souls from the breaths of the living that float all around us in the air. They are way more powerful than the souls from the dying. In fact, they are so strong, they can give White Eye the one thing he wants more than anything else. Life."

I scratched my ear. And then my knee. "If he was alive then he wouldn't have to kill for the souls no more. If we gave him Wah then it could cure his murdering ways!" I said, sitting up straight.

Maymay shook her head. "If he gets the necklace, yes, he will live again. But we must prevent this at all cost."

"I don't right understand what could be worse than him stealing souls?" I muttered.

"If he is alive his curse will come true, Twister."

"He'd do that? He'd kill all the children?" I gasped.

151

Maymay's silence told me everything I needed to know.

I jumped up. The stone dropped to the ground. That would mean Beam would be in danger! My insides burned with anger. And what 'bout the kids at school? They weren't exactly my friends but that didn't mean I wanted any harm to come to them. I'd seen what grief had done to poor old Turrety Knocks and I wouldn't wish that on anyone.

I paced up and down and up and down. Dust rose up from the ground.

"What if we just hid Wah for a bit longer? Until White Eye's body falls to pieces. I've waited months to find Pa, another few weeks wouldn't matter."

Maymay sure looked odd when she smiled. As if it didn't right sit natural on her face. "My spirit guides have told me White Eye is closing in. He knows magic is hiding Wah from him. It won't take him much longer to figure out I'm involved in this. The time to take action is now."

I kicked at the stone. It scuffed the tip of my boot.

"Why would White Eye kill me?"

"In order for him to harness Wah's powers, he has to deceive the necklace into thinking he is you. He'll do that by stealing your soul."

Maymay sure wasn't one to break bad news gently. My guts felt as though they'd been squashed flat under a truck. How could something so awful become even worse than you ever could have imagined?

A bleak thought crossed my mind. "I really don't stand a chance against White Eye, do I?"

"Probably not," Maymay shrugged.

I glared at her.

"The truth upsets you," she said. "Always be grateful for it, for it's rare to come by."

Maymay studied a lampwhittle bird wading in the pond. "It don't matter what I think; it's what you believe that's important. Use Wah wisely and you've the chance to end the mystery of what happened to your pa and banish White Eye to the spirit plane for ever. Use it carelessly and many lives will be lost."

If ever I was tempted to run off screaming into the woods, now would have been as good a time as any.

Maymay patted the step beside her. "Come and sit. There are some things I must tell you 'bout him and I need you to listen carefully. For starters, his right eye is white and he carries a stick."

That wasn't much use. It matched the description

of most of the old folks in the Goodwill Home of Tranquillity.

"But if he's stolen a soul he can change into whatever he took it from," added Maymay.

"You mean if he stole the soul of a big old hairy goat, he'd appear as a big old hairy goat?" I asked.

"Yes," Maymay replied, all matter of fact.

White Eye could be anything or anyone!

"This means you'll have to watch out for certain clues like a person behaving in a strange manner or an animal acting out of character. For instance, a normally shy creature – such as a deer, approaching you with no fear. As soon as you've asked Wah for help, White Eye will pick up on the necklace's energy. He'll know where you are and he'll come for you. You must be on your guard at all times." Maymay turned to me. "As I mentioned earlier, the necklace will turn cold if White Eye is close by."

Words thudded inside my skull like buzzy-flies in a shook-up jar. I seen Clem Hussable's face again. Leering at me with the rusty knife.

Maymay tapped me on the knee. "I want you here with me, not lost in your thoughts," she said. Once she was satisfied she'd my full attention, she spoke again.

"When you become Wah's owner the necklace will do everything in its power to protect you. White Eye can't just appear and kill you for it and he knows this. If he did Wah would simply turn to ash and be of no use to him. Whatever you do be careful to keep it close to you at all times; this will mean there will be only two ways White Eye can take the necklace from you. He will either trick you into giving it to him or he'll take you somewhere the living can't be found. If there ain't no soul in the air, Wah will be useless to you."

Deep furrows appeared on my brow.

Maymay softened her voice. "The necklace is a wonderful gift. Wah will show you a world where anything is possible. You'll have an insight into and be a part of everything that lives and breathes on our planet. It'll be enlightening and exhilarating, but most of all it will help you find your pa."

Pa. It was amazing to think that I would stop seeing him in my memories and I'd start seeing him for real again.

"And don't forget the most important thing of all: Wah has chosen you," she reminded me. Maymay took a teeny-tiny bottle out of her dress pocket and handed it to me.

"What's this?" I asked, peering at the brown liquid sloshing around inside it.

"Whippertonk Water. It's a mixture of sage, rowan, nettle, mountain stream and tequila."

"What am I supposed to do with it?"

"Use it to ward off evil spirits."

"Evil spirits?"

"Evil spirits are like door-to-door salesmen. They always show up at the worst time, are full of bad intentions and can be impossible to get rid of. Sprinkle some of this on them, and they'll be gone in an instant."

"This whole thing really ain't a prank, is it?" I said.

Maymay pulled her shawl around her. Her voice turned prickly as sea urchins. "You should know Wah trusts you and that in turn you must trust the necklace. But I warn you, be extremely careful which souls you take."

"Could you manage a couple of eggs, Twist? Peckers laid them especially for you this morning. And I've got some freshly squeezed orange juice with the pulpy bits in it," said Aunt Honey. "Just the way you like it."

I wished she had a pot of Silver Cloudtip tea. My

shoulders felt even heavier today, as if someone invisible was standing on them.

"Did you sleep OK?" asked Aunt Honey, packing jam jars into boxes.

"I did," I lied. It'd been hard trying to stop my mind from whirring when I returned home from Maymay's. I'd been careful to hide Wah. Then I'd sat by the window watching the sun chase the night away.

I reached down to stroke Point but my hand sailed through the air. My heart sank like a rock in water.

Aunt Honey brought the orange juice over. "Drink up. It'll stop you from getting scurvy and bow legs. Your ma's meeting with the Goodwill Home of Tranquillity tomorrow. She's busy figuring out what's she's going to say to them so that they'll buy all of her jam. I told her she should swear it'll improve stiff joints 'cause everyone'll be running to the breakfast table in the morning to get some." Aunt Honey hooted. "And on the subject of jam, I'm 'bout to drop some off at Hec Bartle's. Want to come with me? Don't tell your ma but you could have three scoops of ice cream at the Fountain if you want."

Aunt Honey was only trying to take my mind off

Point. But I had other plans. Today, I was going to find Pa.

"Thanks, Aunt Honey, but I'd rather stay."

"What'll you do?"

"Get some fresh air."

"Twister, could you keep to the farm?"

"Why?"

"We're concerned 'bout Clem Hussable."

"You needn't be. He'll be busy troubling the other kids at school."

Aunt Honey sat down beside me. Her eyes were the colour of caramel and olives and walnuts. They stared deep into mine. "Had he been picking on you? Is that the reason he was in the barn?"

If I told her he'd threatened to kill me, she and Ma would never let me out of their sights again.

"He didn't bother me any more than he bothered any of the other kids," I said.

Aunt Honey watched to see if I touched my nose. She said that was a sure sign someone was telling a lie. She placed both her hands on the table, palms up.

"What I can't figure out is why Clem did that to Point?" she said.

"He tried to steal a chicken and Point went for him."

"But he wasn't an aggressive dog. His backside never stayed still 'cause he was always wagging that tail of his."

My eyes found the floor. "Clem tried to leave the barn, but I blocked his way. So, he pushed me. Point came to my defence and bit him, and Clem ... well ... he ... what happened is entirely my fault."

Aunt Honey gave a sharp sniff. "Don't you go blaming yourself, do you hear me? He's out of control like his pa. I've got a bad feeling 'bout him in my waters," she said. "I could stay and keep you company?"

"I'd rather be on my own."

"Promise you'll keep to the farm?"

"I'll not go far," I said.

"If Hack or Clem Hussable show face, you run and tell your ma. And make sure all the doors and windows are locked while you're at it." Aunt Honey hesitated. She was in three minds 'bout something. I could tell.

"You go, Aunt Honey. I'll be fine, honestly I will." I even managed a quarter-hearted smile. "And I promise I won't interrupt Ma – unless I really have to."

"Very well." Aunt Honey brought two boiled eggs over to the table and a plate of warm, buttery toast. "There will come a day when all this don't hurt so much; I promise."

A sad thought entered my head. If White Eye came for me this afternoon, I might not see Aunt Honey ever again.

"You're the best aunt I ever had," I blurted out.

Aunt Honey paused for a split-moment. "I know," she said with another sniff as she left with the box of jam.

As soon as Aunt Honey turned into a small dust cloud on the road, I raced up the stairs. I brought the necklace out from under the floorboards and slipped it into my pocket. My fingers tingle-tangled.

The black rooster on the barn refused to move. If the soul in the air really did exist, it would be sure to be floating around on Black Smoke Hill. It was so high up, there was always a breeze blowing at the top.

I left the farm and hurried along Raging River. The bees and birds and buzzy-flies and crickets and cicadas were doing all the gossiping today.

Black Smoke Hill felt even steeper without Point. When I finally reached the top, I sat on a tree stump. I'd left my breath at the bottom of the hill and had to wait some until it catched back up with me.

I missed Point something terrible. Nothing was the

same without him. Me and him had the best day flying the kite; I could still hear my laughter and his barking echoing around the place. It was as if our joy made a mark in the air, like a boot print done in mud.

I brought Wah out from my pocket. It shone bright in the sun. I wondered if the whole of Culleroy seen it flashing in the light. A take-your-breath-away day star.

The thought of White Eye gave me the jeebie-heebies. But Maymay said if I used Wah wisely, I could find Pa and banish White Eye to the spirit plane. Thing is, how do you use a necklace wisely?

I put Wah on over my head. The necklace was warm and tickled as spider silk done when it trailed across your skin. I straightened up the copper face and a surge of energy raced through me. Though it could have been nerves. Maymay said all I had to do was ask Wah for what I wanted. I breathed in deep until my lungs felt fit to burst.

"Show me where Pa is," I said.

I could see Misty Peaks and Culleroy and Holler Woods and Raging River. I could see scuttling beetles and darting lizards and lines of ants and bouncing rabbits and soaring birds and leaping leafhoppers. But I couldn't see Pa.

I stood up and ran round and round and round. If someone had clapped eyes on me, they'd have thought I was loopy loo-loo. When my legs wobbled and the world spun, I stopped to check if Pa had appeared. But there wasn't nobody here except for me.

Perhaps I'd find the soul higher up?

I climbed a pignut hickory tree, surprising a yellow-crested tailwagger, which shrieked and sent leaves flying with its wings. I edged my way along a thick branch. The ground seemed awful far away. I gripped on tight with my legs and raised my arms up towards the heavens, like some folks done at church. Aunt Honey said this happened when people were having an epiphany. I didn't right understand what one of them was, but it sure sounded exciting. I closed my eyes.

"Where is my pa?" I asked. When I opened my eyes, I seen white flashing lights dancing in front of them. Were these the souls? As soon as I blinked, the dots vanished. I must have squeezed my eyes shut too hard.

I climbed back down and threw myself on to the grass. There was no such thing as soul in the air! And Wah's face wasn't even moving like it had the last time. Maymay must have pulled the cotton over my eyes. Pa had been right warning me to stay away from her. She'd got me good with her spooky words and witchy ways. Thing is, was she even a medicine woman? Aunt Honey always talked 'bout the travelling pedlars who used to pass through Culleroy when she was a girl. They'd be all tall hats and green bottles and silvery tongues and hooded eyes. For a high price, they claimed their tinctures could cure everything from itchy rashes to limping limbs. But Aunt Honey said their potions were only good for one thing: oiling squeaky barn doors. She said if something seemed too good to be true, it was probably just that. Kinda like a piece of jewellery that would know where a man was who'd been missing for months. And Maymay throwing White Eye into the mix and making me believe the story 'bout him was true? Was this another one of her stupid tests to see if I had guts? But then again, how'd she got me to fly up on to her roof yesterday? Maybe floating was a side-effect of a broken heart. Aunt Honey swore grief done strange things to people. I mean, just look at Turrety Knocks. He was so sad he drank too much and lived in a shack made out of junk.

A strong breeze cuffed the grass. The trees shifted

uncomfortably. My hope of seeing Pa escaped from me the same way air done from a punctured tyre.

I put the necklace back into my pocket and wandered down towards Cedar Creek Lake. I stripped the seeds off grass stems and tore leaves up into green confetti. My hands were sticky and bitter with leaf juice.

Cedar Creek Lake was playing a game to see how long it could keep still for. I found some flat stones and skimmed them across the water. They broke the grey clouds that lay on the lake's surface and made the trees and the sky shiver. Small rings rippled out, turning into bigger rings. They reminded me of the smoke rings from Maymay's pipe. I'd wanted to put my finger through them. I should have poked her in her always-crying eye instead. I could hear her voice in my head now. *It's what you believe that's important; you must trust the necklace.*

I stopped throwing stones.

Did I believe in myself? And did I really trust Wah?

I sighed. I didn't right think I trusted either Maymay or Wah.

Aunt Honey said you should always focus on what you want in your life, not on what you don't want. I couldn't save Point. But I could make Ma better again if I found

Pa. Perhaps I ought to give Wah one more chance? Forget 'bout my doubts and really believe the necklace would help me this time. I took Wah back out of my pocket and put it on. It felt icy cool against my clammy skin.

The sun got shy and snuck behind the clouds.

An uneasy feeling crept over me. The hairs went up on my arms.

A strong gust of wind blew in. Trees groaned and branches snapped. Leaves gathered on the ground and rushed away from the lake like a pack of scared animals. The wind hit my face and stole my breath.

A rotten tree on the island fallen into Cedar Creek Lake. Next to it, a tall dark figure leant on a stick.

I froze.

White Eye wasn't an old spooky tale. He was real. And watching my every move. I'd used the necklace, hadn't I? White Eye had come to get me.

I tucked Wah under my T-shirt and ran as fast as a mountain hare being hunted by an eagle. The thought of White Eye on my tail wasn't a good one.

I sprinted back up towards Black Smoke Hill, too scared to look behind me. I couldn't hear no footsteps 'cause I was panting so loud. I flashed past the oaks and the hickories at the top of the hill and fled down the steep path to Raging River. Behind me, two crows cried out in fear. I didn't stop.

Thunder boomed in the distance. Aunt Honey said thunder wasn't really thunder. It was Great-Aunt Bonnie moving her furniture around in heaven. Great-Aunt Bonnie must sit on huge chairs to make all that racket.

I shot out of the trees. Raging River rushed by all bruised. Boy! Was I glad to see it! I'd be home soon. I hurried along the rocky path. Rabbits scattered and birds fled and buzzy-flies zoomed and beetles scuttled and ants swarmed.

I skidded to a halt, gasping for breath. Clem Hussable was up ahead, crouching over a lifeless skunk. He poked at it with a stick. A crow had pinched its eyes. I smelled burnt tyre and sickly sweet grass and rotten eggs.

The light dimmed even further as my heart sank. Clem was out of school early! He sensed he was being watched. When he spied me, he moved the same way a cat done when it don't want to scare off its prey.

"And to think I thought it smelled bad," he said, booting the skunk. A cloud of buzzy-flies rose from it. The skunk rolled on to the riverbank, leaving behind a dark stain on the grass. Clem wiped his snotty nose on a shabby sleeve. My muscles tensed. He spat. There was a storm brewing on the inside of him 'cause his knuckles were white.

"I took Hack's knife 'cause I left mine at yours. Thing

is, Miss Ida catched me showing it to Gordy Sedge. She told me to leave and never come back. Happens she's done me a favour 'cause school was a waste of my time anyways. Hack ain't going to be too pleased she's kept his favourite knife. I ought to stick one in him too." The lightning flashing was the only brightness in Clem's eyes.

My eyes flicked to the trees. If I went back to Black Smoke Hill, there could be worse things than Clem Hussable waiting in there for me. And if I plunged into Raging River, I'd be swept away like a leaf.

"Don't even think 'bout running, Twister, I'd be on you in a flash."

Lightning shattered the sky. Clem scrambled down to the riverbank. He grabbed two rocks and leapt up on to the path.

"I'll make it look as if you had an accident. They'll think you slipped and banged your head and drowned in the river."

Clem weighed the rocks in his hands to see which one was the heaviest. "You should have seen Tilly Bluer when they dragged her out last summer. The fish had chewed her lips off and she'd swelled up to the size of a bloated hog." Clem let go of one of the rocks. It landed with a heavy thud. The trees stopped thrashing around. They were scared stiff too.

"No use closing your eyes. You might as well see the end coming, same as your dog done," said Clem.

My breath was shallow. Sweat trickled down my face. I couldn't move not one muscle. I opened my eyes back up.

The clouds above started to cry, their tears washing away the colours of the land.

Clem stepped closer.

I gritted my teeth. Point had been brave at the end. I would be too.

I thought 'bout him and Pa and Ma and Aunt Honey and Beam and Turrety Knocks. Strange thing was my guts unclenched. The fear melted away and a calm feeling spread through my body. I accepted what was going to happen.

I swear I heard a thousand voices chanting. But it was hard to tell over the din of Raging River.

Clem cocked his head. "Ain't you even going to scream? You're so dull, it's killing *me*."

Wah started to tingle-tangle. I'd forgotten it was there. My hands flew up to my neck. The discs felt orange-coal hot. A jolt of energy shocked me into action.

I yelled out, "I need fighting strength!"

Clem flinched, dropping the rock. "You're even crazier than I thought," he muttered.

All of a sudden, hundreds of bubbles appeared in the air around us. They were clear and 'bout the size of giant gobstoppers. One smacked right off Clem's head. I rubbed my eyes.

There was a blue whale inside it!

This had to be the soul Maymay had been talking 'bout.

A breeze blew in, bringing even more bubbles with it. Clem didn't say not one word 'bout them, even though they were right under his nose.

"Look, Clem! Do you see that penguin?" I said, pointing over to the gum tree.

"Thought you were supposed to see weird stuff *after* you've been hit on the head," Clem muttered, glancing behind him. "Stop trying to distract me. It won't work."

He couldn't see the soul bubbles. He really couldn't.

Clem bent down to pick the rock back up.

A reindeer raced past me. It shook its antlers and snorted. I laughed. If Beam had been here she'd be jumping for joy and clapping her hands. I wanted to leap after the bubbles and catch them in my hands. I longed to find out what was in each and every one of them. I had never seen anything so wonderful in my life!

A fish bounced off my arm. It was all teeth and bug-eyes and sharp spines and puffing gills.

The discs on the necklace burned. A white bubble shot through the trees towards me. I heard a creaking noise. To my amazement Wah's copper mouth opened wide. It swallowed the soul bubble in one giant gulp!

I felt chilly. My teeth hurt. I could even taste the cold. Like the first lick of a strawberry ice-lolly don't taste of strawberry. It tasted of ice.

Every bone in my body grumbled and cracked. My guts lurched.

Clem straightened back up.

I fallen to the ground in agony. Clem took one look at me and gasped.

I smelled the dead skunk. But I also smelled fish hugging the riverbank and birds in the bushes and dragonflies on the underside of the reeds and voles in their holes and curled-up foxes and trembling deer.

I smelled Clem's scabs and snot and greasy hair. I could even smell what lay warm and tasty under his skin.

Clem's eyes widened.

172

I was different.

Powerful.

Fearless.

Ferocious.

I heard Clem's heartbeat quicken. He hurled the rock at me. It catched the side of my head. He turned to flee. Seeing him running triggered something deep within me. I bounded after him.

I was on four legs and covered in a thick coat of white and grey fur.

I was a wolf.

Clem tripped and fallen. The scent of fresh blood filled my nose. He tried to crawl away from me, but I pulled him back with my teeth. He rolled over and lashed out. His fists struck my face as I tore at his sleeve.

I moved forward, standing over him. His neck arched, soft and smooth. I knew one bite would make him still.

His hands shot up to my throat. His dirty nails clawed at it. Fur flew. Before I could stop myself, I bit him. I raised my head to strike again but I catched a strange scent in the air. I heard the squelch of footsteps in the distance. Instinct told me to be afraid. Danger was coming.

Clem's eyes were closed. One side of his face ran red in the rain.

I wobbled to my feet, my muscles aching and my jaw throbbing. The fur had disappeared. My sense of smell dulled and I could no longer hear Clem's heartbeat.

I limped along Ranging River, fast as I could. The rain darkened my clothes. The leaves in the trees twitched and jerked. Crows huddled with their backs turned. Thunder shook the sky and the ground. The gathering puddles of cloud-tears quivered.

I looked around to check if I was being followed. But I wasn't. I hurried along past the bridge and took the path to the gate. Aunt Honey must still be in town 'cause the truck wasn't back yet.

I'd asked for fighting strength and Wah had given me the soul of a wolf! I should have been much more careful. What had I done to Clem?

When I entered the house, it was hushety-quiet; Ma must be resting. I catched sight of myself in the hallway mirror. My hair was black and flat and dripping, there were streaks of dirt on my face and red scratches on my neck. Dark shadows hung under my eyes.

My mouth fallen open.

My eyes weren't my own blue eyes any more. They were yellow wolf eyes.

I leapt back from the mirror.

That's when I noticed the necklace had vanished.

The truck squealed to a halt in the yard.

"Twister?" Aunt Honey hollered up from the kitchen. "You here? Twisterrrr!"

I shut my eyes tight and pulled the covers over my head.

The stairs creaked and the door burst open. Aunt Honey marched over to my bedside. Her hand shook my shoulder. I third-opened one eye. Aunt Honey had a deep crease between hers. "If it ain't sleeping beauty! What on earth's that?" she asked.

"What?"

"Is that a bump on your forehead?"

I opened both my eyes. Aunt Honey didn't run off screaming in terror. The wolf's eyes must have vanished! "I slipped in the mud."

"Your Great-Uncle Cee once broke his arm skidding on a grape. I think you've inherited his natural flair for acrobatics," said Aunt Honey, holding up her hand. "How many fingers can you count?"

"Three," I said.

"You're not concussed," said Aunt Honey. "Otherwise you'd be seeing double."

Clem on the path and the missing necklace came flooding back to me.

"I ain't feeling so well," I said.

"I knew I should have stayed home," said Aunt Honey. "However, it just so happens I've got the best cure for sniffles, coughs, scrapes, bumps and general malaise on the stove. Tomato-herby soup. It'll put hairs on your chest." Aunt Honey left the room and clattered down the stairs.

That wasn't funny 'cause I'd already had hair on my chest today. Wolf hair.

What if Clem was dead? I'd wanted to protect myself from him but no way had I meant to kill him. It was Clem who was the murderer. Not me. Taking the soul had changed me into something I couldn't control. Something dangerous.

One thing was for sure: I was going to have to go back for him and the necklace. Clem must have torn it off clawing at my neck. Wah would be lying somewhere in the mud. But what if that had been White Eye's footsteps I'd heard? If he had the necklace all he'd have to do is finish me off in order to use its powers. He'd know where I was now too. And if he came for me tonight, I'd no way of protecting myself.

The door flew open. I jumped and the windows rattled and the posters fluttered and the books flapped shut. Aunt Honey entered with a tray. She placed it in front of me and tucked a napkin under my chin. The tomato-herby soup was bright red. I thought of Clem on the path.

"Aunt Honey, I think another walk would make me feel better."

"You've just had one. Are you OK? You got yourself a fever?"

Aunt Honey leant forward and clamped a hand over my forehead.

"You're clammy, but you'll live."

I winced. I might not for much longer with White Eye after me.

"You're not going out, Twist. It's raining cats and dogs."

I peered out the window but I couldn't see none. You'd think cats and dogs falling from the sky would make a heck of a racket.

"Besides, you're in no fit state," she added. Aunt Honey sat on the bed making everything on the tray slide towards her. "Careful, Twist!" she said as she settled herself. "Hec Bartle was right pleased when I dropped off the jam. But get this – who should walk into the store but Miss Ida. She was all flustered 'cause she catched Clem Hussable waving a knife around in class. So, she expelled him – 'bout time too if you ask me. He ain't going back to school!"

If he was lying dead on the path he wouldn't be going anywhere. Before I could confess to her what'd happened at Raging River, Aunt Honey leapt in. "When I left the store, there was quite a crowd gathering outside Doc Winters's surgery. I trotted over to see what was happening and guess what? Clem was attacked this afternoon! And who should find him but Turrety Knocks! He fetched Jink Rilla and they drove him to Doc's. Clem's real lucky they didn't fling him into the river."

Clem was alive! My guts relaxed some. It must have been Turrety Knocks's footsteps I'd heard on the path!

Aunt Honey pinched a piece of bread and dunked it into the tomato-herby soup. "There's more. Hack Hussable turned up drunk!"

"Is Clem OK?" I asked.

"Doc thinks he should get the sight back in his eye, but his face will be scarred for life. You ain't eating, Twist."

"I lost my appetite."

"Go on, take a spoonful for your Aunt Honey."

I tried a teeny-tiny taste. Satisfied, Aunt Honey continued on. "All of a sudden there were raised voices and Doc chucked Hack out on to the street. Hack was cussing and swore there'd be retribution for what happened to his boy. You should have seen the look he gave me." Aunt Honey's eyes were as round as plates.

"What does red-tree-boo-shon mean?"

"The word's *retribution*. It means revenge. Turrety Knocks left Doc's not long after. He was fuming. I offered him a lift home, so he wouldn't be tempted to stop off at the liquor store. He said when Clem came around on Doc's table, he'd told them it'd been *you* who'd attacked him!"

My face changed the same colour as the soup.

"You OK?"

I nodded.

"The lying gutter rat! Thank goodness Doc wouldn't listen to him. He said Clem must be confused on account of his injuries. Doc insisted you were too small to have inflicted such wounds and concluded the scratches and bites were consistent with a wolf attack. Hack wouldn't buy it though. That's when Doc snapped – he told him to sober up and slung him out on his ear. Thing is, Hack's on the warpath now. This ain't over by a long shot." Aunt Honey reached around me to plump up the pillows. "I tell you, when Clem gets better, I'll wring his neck with my own hands."

Aunt Honey stole another chunk of bread and chewed it real fast. "We need to be extra careful in case Hack comes here looking for trouble." She got off the bed and took the tray. "But don't you worry 'bout a thing. You're exhausted. You'll feel as good as new if you get some sleep."

I nodded. My eyelids grew heavy. Hack Hussable was the least of my worries right now. I'd find Wah in a little while when I didn't feel so darn tired.

I woke with a start. I lay still as drain pipes, but my ears couldn't hear nothing. I checked each and every one of the shadows for White Eye before I got up.

It sure did hurt some standing. I hobbled over to the window and opened it. The sun had wearied and gone to bed; hundreds of stars winked at me. The night air rushed in and I breathed deep, trying not to think 'bout which souls were bouncing around in it.

I looked up to the silver field where Point lay. I longed for him to be here with me, all twitching paws and soft woofs as he chased the rabbits in his dreams. That was when I noticed the windows in the barn were lit up bright yellow. I'd never seen the barn glow like that before. Hairs rose up on the back of my neck.

White Eye had found me!

My heart beat so fast I felt light-headed. I cursed myself for losing Wah and for falling asleep when I should have been out hunting for the necklace. There was no other thing for it: I had to face him 'cause I would not put Ma and Aunt Honey in danger.

I threw on some clothes and crept down the stairs to the kitchen. Something brushed against my leg and I nearly cried out with the fright of it.

Mew purred and flashed her big marmalade eyes at me. "You stay here, Mew," I ordered, grabbing a rolling pin from the pantry.

I unlocked the kitchen door. My teeth chittered. I felt queasy.

The yard was sticky with mud. I stopped and shook myself, much the same as Mew done after a nap. I couldn't face White Eye with a foggy head: I'd have to have my wits 'bout me.

I took a deep breath and slid into the barn. I hadn't been in here since ... well, since what had happened to Point. The place made my heart shrink.

The yellow light had vanished. The moon peeped in through the window on the roof. I smelled straw and cow pee-pee and pitch and oil-soaked wood and cocooned buzzy-flies and dust and earth and rust and damp and cold iron.

Gripping tightly on to the rolling pin, I edged forward.

I felt a tap on my shoulder. I yelled and spun round, poised to attack, and stared right into a familiar pair of eyes. I dropped the rolling pin, which landed on my foot.

"Hello, Twistie!" she said.

"Beam!" I said through gritted teeth as my toes throbbed. "You near scared the life away from me again!"

"You're a deep sleeper. I've been chucking stones at your window for ages. Surprised the noise didn't wake the dead. Um – were you going to hit me with that rolling pin?"

"I thought you were someone else."

"And who would that be?" she asked, cocking her head.

I couldn't very well tell her I'd thought she was White Eye.

"It's a little late to be paying me a visit," I said.

"Aw! Don't be like that." She grinned. Her teeth were as white as icing on a wedding cake.

"Anything to tell me?" she asked, twirling her hair around her finger.

Was that a hint of anger in her voice?

There was no way I could confess to Beam I'd taken Wah. She'd never forgive me. I'd have to keep that from her at all cost.

I picked at a rag nail. "Nothing new."

"Really?" Beam lifted her frilly skirts, climbed on to some straw bales and plonked herself down. Her legs swung forward and backwards, hitting off the straw. Dust flew up, making me sneeze.

Her shoulders slumped. "I thought we were friends, Twistie?"

I started to feel uneasy. "We are."

"Best friends tell each other 99.9% *everything*." She folded her arms and scowled at me.

"What's all this 'bout? Come on, spit it out," I said.

"Maymay's not happy with you either. What did you do?"

My face fallen. Did Maymay know 'bout me taking the soul of the wolf? And if she knew that, did she know 'bout me attacking Clem and losing the necklace too? Aunt Honey said if you're not sure how to reply to a question, you were best to answer it by asking another question.

"She real mad?" I asked.

"Mad as a bear that's been shot at by a hunter and then stung on the backside by a whole forest of wild bees."

That sure was angry.

"Maymay says you've got to be more careful."

I narrowed my eyes. "How does she know?"

"Maymay knows everything. Question is, what do you have to be more careful 'bout?"

I gulped. Beam knew full well what I'd done. I barely recognised her without a smile on her face.

"I'm sorry, Beam. I had to take the necklace. I've never felt as wretched as I do now, I miss Point so much it feels like my heart's been ripped out. Nothing will ever make up for his loss, but having Pa back will make life more bearable. And he'll make Ma better again."

Beam stayed silent as prayers.

I could hardly hear her voice when she finally decided to speak. "Maymay wanted me to warn you that White Eye's in Holler Woods."

A cloud hugged the moon. For a split-moment Beam disappeared in the shadows. I felt her shiver. "And another thing," she said. "Maymay's gone."

My eyes flooded. I swallowed hard until the barn stopped rippling. Maymay knew I didn't stand a chance against White Eye, her spirit guides would have told her so. That was why she'd fled, so she could save her own skin. How could she! She'd left me all on my own at a time I needed her the most. What a fool I'd been to trust her. I should never have taken Wah. Beam snapped me out of my thoughts.

"You mentioned a necklace, but you didn't say that it was White Eye who was the catch." Beam jumped down from the bales. Her skin turned paler than china cups. "What were you thinking of? Everyone knows he's a bad man, Twistie. A real bad man."

"I think I've been stupid," I said.

"You don't say!" Her words hurt more than slaps.

"But there's a chance, and it's a teeny-tiny one, that I could beat White Eye and save a lot of lives. I have to take it." I didn't want to tell her life might be in danger 'cause White Eye planned on killing all the children. She was upset enough as it was.

"Ain't you heard the stories? You can't go up against him! You'll die," she yelled. "Whatever Maymay has told you is wrong."

"I think it's best if you don't see me no more." My throat tightened as I fought back tears. It was not what I wanted to say 'cause I'd lose her for sure. And right now she was the only friend I had. It was my fault Point had died. If Beam stayed away from me, I sure as heck could keep her safe from White Eye.

Beam's bottom lip trembled. "You mean that, Twistie?"

I nodded, too upset to speak.

"I'm sorry I was rude earlier. It's just 'cause I care. Hope you know that."

I shrugged, avoiding her eyes.

"I've got something for you. It's from Maymay." Beam's voice sounded broken.

"Don't want nothing from her."

"Would you just listen to me this once, you stubborn fool?" She stamped her foot. "I don't want to but I *have* to give it to you, so take it is what you'll do. Promise me one last thing and I'll never bother you again," she said.

"OK, what?"

"There's an old man who lives next to the river, not far from here."

"Turrety Knocks?"

"Will you look out for him?"

I sighed. "Has he been drinking again?"

"Will you?"

I thought 'bout Turrety Knocks's moss and bark eyes and Pa's letter that he'd kept safe for me.

"Of course," I said.

"Thank you. Here, you'll need this." She placed something soft in my hand. "I guess this is goodbye then."

I unwrapped the cloth she'd handed me. Inside was Wah. All coppery and orange and warm and beautiful. My fingers tingle-tangled. It took my breath away. When I looked up to say goodbye, she had gone.

The clouds must have cried themselves happy 'cause they were white again. Sunbeams stretched across the room to touch me, as if we were 'bout to play a game of tag.

Everything came flooding back to me. My heart lurched. Maymay had gone. Beam too. White Eye was closing in on me and I was all alone. Except for Wah. Aunt Honey always told me to be grateful for what I've got, and I was. Having the necklace back meant I still had a chance of finding Pa.

I heard the truck screech to a halt in the yard. Seconds later, the kitchen door crashed open. "Twister!" hollered Aunt Honey. "Get down here!"

I leapt out of bed and rushed to the window. Turrety Knocks lay flat out in the back of the truck.

I raced down the stairs.

Mew shot past me with her tail between her legs.

"Twist, you're going to have to help me carry Turrety Knocks. He's hurt real bad."

I hurried out to him.

"Grab his legs. We'll pick him up after three: one, two, three," she said.

Aunt Honey and I lifted Turrety Knocks and took him into the house.

"Can you make it to the downstairs bedroom?" asked Aunt Honey through clenched teeth.

"Yup," I gasped.

I flung myself against the door to open it. We staggered into the room and laid him down on the bed.

"Fetch some water and disinfectant," barked Aunt Honey.

Turrety Knocks's face shone purple and black and red. His moss and bark eyes hid under swollen skin. His clothes were torn and muddy. I sprinted upstairs to the bathroom and grabbed some cotton balls and a towel and a bottle of disinfectant, then hurried to the kitchen and poured some water into a bowl.

Back in the bedroom, I watched as Aunt Honey flung the window open. She removed Turrety Knocks's flappy shirt and gently placed a pillow under his head. She then unscrewed the lid off the disinfectant and poured some into the bowl. It turned the water milky and chased every other smell out of my nostrils with its sharp scent. She dabbed at Turrety Knocks's face. The cotton ball changed from white to red. Aunt Honey's brow came down low.

"What happened?" I asked.

"I found him by the side of the road. Someone seen fit to tear his shack apart. They tried to do the same to him too."

"Who'd do such a thing?" I cried.

Aunt Honey stopped cleaning his cuts. She placed two fingers across his wrist and sat still as rails, as if she was listening to something deep inside him.

"He needs to see Doc," she said.

"Want to put him back in the truck?"

"His body ain't going to suffer another pummelling from the road. I'll have to fetch Doc and your ma while I'm at it. Of all the times for her to be with the Goodwill Home of Tranquillity. Thing is, I don't want to leave you on your own."

I remembered the promise I'd made to Beam. "I'll take care of him. I'll clean his cuts and make sure he's comfortable. If he wakes, I'll give him water," I said.

"Well then, he'll be in mighty good hands." Aunt Honey came over to me. "Try not to worry; this loon is as tough as old boots. Whatever you do, don't open the door to no one, especially if there's a maniac on the loose. I'll be as quick as I can." She patted my arm before hurrying out the room.

Turrety Knocks didn't move. I was used to seeing him lying still by the church, except there weren't no brown bottles at his side this time.

The truck started up and roared out of the yard.

I dipped a cotton ball into the water and cleaned the cuts on Turrety Knocks's hands. His fingers were thick and bent on account of all the hard work he'd done. The dirt washed away and I seen the blue worms under his skin again. I couldn't imagine his hands being nimble enough to fix the kite. But fix it they had.

Turrety Knocks's breathing was shallow. As if a weight on his chest was stopping him from drawing air into his lungs. Where he wasn't dark from punches and kicks, his skin was as pale as church candles. His lips were losing their berry colour.

His hands were folded across his chest. He was wearing a wedding ring. I'd never noticed it before. I picked up his arm and placed my ear over his heart. It was silent. I laid his arm back down.

I couldn't just sit back and do nothing. That's when it struck me faster than a trout snatching a mayfly on a summer's evening. I could ask Wah to save Turrety Knocks's life.

The black rooster on the barn twirled and the trees shook the crows. I reckoned there would be plenty of soul floating around in the yard.

I wiped the sweat from my palms.

Using the necklace might bring White Eye to the farm. But I just had to do what I could to save Turrety

Knocks. Thing is, I'd nearly killed Clem yesterday. What if I asked Wah for the wrong soul and finished Turrety Knocks off? But if his heart had stopped beating, he was a goner anyway.

As soon as I put Wah on, every nerve in my body wriggled.

I closed my eyes and pictured Turrety Knocks giving me the kite. I thought 'bout flying it on Black Smoke Hill with Point – I heard him barking and me laughing.

My heart opened and grew with every beat. I breathed slow and steady. The noises of the farm faded.

"Thank you for helping me save Turrety Knocks's life." I shouted it out so loud, Gorgeous George flapped and Proudfoot snorted and Swayback heaved himself out of his mud bath.

Wah burned around my neck. I was pretty sure I heard a thousand voices chanting. Swirls of bubbles poured down over the barn roof and bounced up off the ground. I gasped at the sight of them.

A bubble got stuck in my hair. I gave it a push.

A lion was inside it! All rippy-flesh teeth and wild mane and buzzy-flies and lichen-coloured eyes and nose scars. It roared fierce. I clapped my hand over the mouth of the necklace. Not in a month of Mondays did I want that soul!

"Come on, Wah!" I yelled.

A black bubble whizzed straight towards the necklace. Before I could even guess what was in it, Wah's mouth stretched open. The bubble disappeared inside.

I started to feel hot as a branding iron; my bones throbbed and my muscles tensed. My arms and legs disappeared. Before I could scream, I puffed up like a giant piece of popcorn the size of a shed. I left the ground and floated in the air as every bit of me vibrated.

The yard darkened. Mew arched her back and spat and rushed off towards the vegetable patch.

I catched sight of myself in the window.

I was a storm cloud. A deep anger consumed me. Every. Single. Part. Of. Me. Raged. As I expanded, so did my fury. Hot air rushed around me.

I blotted out the light from the sun. The air crackled. I sped towards the house and slammed against the door. It crashed open. The windows rattled as I billowed into the kitchen. China smashed and chairs fallen over and pots clattered to the floor and knives flew from one end of the room to the other.

I curled wallpaper and upset pictures. I grumbled and

rumbled along the hallway, rushing into the next room. I filled every inch of it with my grey vapours.

Below me lay a body.

I quivered. Sparks flew.

I flickered. A warning.

I boomed so loud the whole house trembled. There was a blinding flash. White jagged lines shot out from me, striking metal. Smoke rose up.

The body on the bed glowed electric blue. And twitched.

18

Water splashed on to my face. The shock of it woke me up.

Two eyes peered down at me. One was moss coloured and the other was bark coloured. "Twister?" he said.

I winced when my heart leapt with joy. Turrety Knocks was alive!

"Twister? You were out cold. You OK?"

I heaved myself up off the floor on to a chair. I dried my face with my sleeve. The room looked as if everything in it had been turned upside down and round and round and inside out. Except for Turrety Knocks. I gawped at him. All the black and purple and red had vanished from his skin. It was as if he'd never been hurt in the first place.

He stared right back at me. "Your hair's standing on end."

I must still have some storm soul inside me. As I flattened it down, sparks shot out from my fingertips. I tucked my hands under my legs – I didn't want to go setting the house on fire. "A bad storm passed overhead," I said. "Are you OK?"

"My wedding ring is scorching hot. Think I got burned." He waggled his hand in the air.

The lightning must have struck the metal ring on his finger and jolted his heart back to life! Wah sure was clever to have chosen that soul.

"I woke with a heck of a start, but apart from that, I feel fifty years younger. Where am I?" he asked.

"Aunt Honey found you at the side of the road. She brought you home and turned tail to fetch Ma and Doc Winters."

"Why?"

"You were hurt bad."

Turrety Knocks's eyes grew smaller. Like he was

searching for a clue at the back of his mind. He let out a sigh. "Don't remember a darn thing."

"Aunt Honey said somebody destroyed your home," I said. My skull throbbed. Even my eyeballs hurt.

"Hope Neeps is all right," he said.

"Neeps?"

"My cat."

I remembered the rusty cat I'd clapped eyes on in his shack. "Aunt Honey says ain't nobody better at finding comfort than a cat."

Turrety Knocks smiled. "Your aunt's a smart lady. I'm sure Neeps will be just fine and talking 'bout being fine – something don't add up here. If I was in such a bad way, how come I'm as fit as a fiddle now?"

I opened my mouth to say something but nothing came out. He wasn't exactly going to believe a lightning strike started his heart again 'cause I'd used a necklace to take the soul of a storm.

Turrety Knocks cocked his head. His hand shot out as if he was 'bout to throttle me. His thick fingers curled around Wah and then let go.

"Tell me you ain't, Twister?" he said, his voice sounding all chilly-icy.

"Ain't what?"

"Ain't used that wretched necklace to help me, that's what!" Turrety Knocks growled.

My mouth fallen open.

"You know 'bout the necklace?" I asked.

Turrety Knocks's eyes filled with fear. "It's cursed, Twister, the necklace is cursed! You've put yourself in grave danger."

"I didn't have no choice: your heart had stopped beating," I said.

Turrety Knocks blinked at me. "I don't understand. I gave the wretched thing to Maymay only yesterday for safekeeping. I'd found it next to Clem at Raging River. How did you get it?"

"She gave it back to me."

"Back to you?" Turrety Knocks kicked off the bed covers and stood up. He pulled his muddy trousers on over his long johns and threw on his raggedy shirt. "I thought Clem had injured himself mucking around with it. But he didn't, did he? You said Maymay gave it back to you, which means you must have had the necklace before I found it. You used it to hurt Clem. He was telling the truth after all!" Spit flew from Turrety Knocks's mouth.

"Clem was going to hit me with a rock and make it look like I'd drowned in the river." My words cooled the heat raging through Turrety Knocks's veins. He sat back down on the bed.

"I guess Clem turned out just the same as Hack," he said.

"The necklace changed me into a wolf so I could protect myself."

"A *wolf*?"

"I didn't mean to hurt him so bad," I said. "It was an accident."

"Clem's lucky to be alive. It was wrong of Maymay to persuade you to use the necklace."

"Pa mentioned her name in the letter you gave me. I reckoned she could be the only person who might know what'd happened to him. Maymay didn't force me to take the necklace. I asked her if I could have it. I thought if I found Pa, Ma would get better and everything could go back to the way it was before he disappeared. Instead, I've gone and made a mess of everything."

Turrety Knocks swallowed hard. "I've been so catched up in my own troubles I ain't been here for you." He stood up. "All that's going to change now. We need to find Maymay; it's time she helped us put things right."

"She left last night."

"She done what?"

"She's gone."

"Why! I know it ain't gentlemanly to be furious with a woman, but I've got to tell you I'm real mad at her now." Turrety Knocks started to put on his boots. "Twister, we're going to have to get away from here. It ain't safe."

"You know 'bout White Eye, don't you?" I whispered.

Turrety Knocks's face fallen. It was a while before he spoke.

"I was mending fencing in the top field. Dug the necklace up. Thought it was scrap at first, but after I cleaned the mud off I knew it was something special. I ain't never seen nothing like it before. It made me think of a story I'd heard when I was a boy 'bout an old necklace in Culleroy that could make your wishes come true." Turrety Knocks continued on. "My wife, Bethy, was sick. Doc Winters told me he couldn't do no more for her. Nobody was around – so I thought what harm could it possibly do to put it on and ask if it could make her better? There ain't nothing I wouldn't have tried if it meant she'd be cured." Turrety Knocks pursed his lips. "A few hours later an old man knocked at the cabin. There was something 'bout his manner I didn't care for and it was odd 'cause it was as if he knew I had the necklace. He said he was a dealer in ancient artefacts and asked if I'd come across any on the land. He mentioned he'd pay a handsome price, particularly for jewellery. I told him I didn't have nothing. The man got angry and swore my lies would cost me." Turrety Knocks's voice trembled. "A fire, Twister. The next day a terrible fire swept through the edge of Holler Woods burning everything in its path." Turrety Knocks breathed in sharp, as if he was there again surrounded by the screams and the smoke and the flames. "You know the rest," he said.

I sucked my breath in. No wonder Turrety Knocks's eyes were so faded. All his tears of grief must have washed the colour out of them.

"I'm so sorry, Turrety Knocks."

"I was sure the man who'd turned up at the cabin was responsible for the fire. I tried tracking him down – he stood out like a sore thumb 'cause one of his eyes was white, but nobody had seen hide nor hair of him. It was only when I got talking to Maymay soon after, that she told me all 'bout the necklace and that White Eye really did exist."

My mouth trembled. "White Eye done all that to you?"

"He did."

"What did you do with the necklace?"

"I had never planned on keeping it 'cause I'd found it on your pa's land, which meant he was its rightful owner, so I gave it to him. He reckoned it belonged to Maymay 'cause her ancestors lived on the land long before your grandpappy done. Thinking of it, that can't have been more than a couple of days before he disappeared."

Maymay had never mentioned she'd met Pa! Why had she lied 'bout that? And what else was she not telling the truth 'bout? Perhaps she'd known where he was all along.

Turrety Knocks's eyes shone bright. "White Eye's evil, Twist, but I'll be darned if he thinks he's going to harm the people I care 'bout again. Pack a bag. If we leave now we'll draw him away and keep your ma and Aunt Honey safe."

Before we could move a muscle, a truck pulled up in the yard.

I took Wah off and put it in my pocket. Turrety Knocks leapt into the bed and pulled the covers around him.

I hobbled to the kitchen, every muscle in my body grumbling. I flung the door open expecting to see Aunt Honey and Ma and Doc Winters.

"I think it's time you and me had a chat 'bout my boy," said Hack Hussable.

I'd been so busy fretting over Turrety Knocks and White Eye, I forgot to worry 'bout Hack!

"Oh, the firecracker's gone all shy on me. Either you come out to discuss this or I'm coming in. Your choice." Hack's voice sounded casual, as if he'd just dropped by for tea and cake.

There was a cut on his cheek. His tongue slid out to lick his cracked lips and slip-slided back into his mouth.

Turrety Knocks shoved past me.

Hack's face fallen for a split-moment. "I must be losing my touch if you're still standing," he sneered.

"You! You trashed my home and left me out for the crows to feed on!" gasped Turrety Knocks.

Hack laughed. He folded his arms and leant against the truck. His clothes flapped in the breeze. That was 'cause there was no flesh for them to cling on to.

"You ain't got no business being here," snapped Turrety Knocks.

"I ain't going nowhere until you 'fess up 'bout what you did to my boy," said Hack.

"What're you talking 'bout?" said Turrety Knocks.

The scar on Hack's neck flushed scarlet. "There ain't no wolf in Culleroy."

Turrety Knocks and I held our breaths.

"It didn't take me long to figure out the two of you are in cahoots. Firecracker asked you to rough up Clem for what he done to her dog. The two of you ambushed him by the river, but it went wrong 'cause you lost control. Heck, maybe even Jink Rilla was in on it too. The only reason you took Clem to Doc's was 'cause if you pretended to save him nobody would suspect that it was you who'd tried to kill him."

"That's garbage, Hack," said Turrety Knocks. "I wouldn't hit a child."

"Of course not. Fire is more your style."

"What are you implying?" Turrety Knocks raised his fists. I pushed past him and squared up to Hack.

"I hurt Clem. Not him. There was no ambush. He's got nothing to do with this and nor has Jink Rilla," I said.

He licked his lips. "Now we're getting somewhere,

Firecracker. But do you expect me to believe you done that to my boy all by yourself?"

"I do. Clem killed my dog and was going to attack me by the river. I acted in self-defence."

"You've a fine imagination, I'll give you that. You trapped my boy in that barn over there and set your hound on him. Your mutt was nothing but a rabid beast and in the eyes of the law Clem was well within his rights destroying a dangerous animal. And after what you and your dog put him through, you'd forgive him for being a little hostile down by Raging River."

"That's a lie! My dog was the gentlest, bravest dog ever. He was protecting me from Clem," I said.

"You calling my boy a liar?" Hack stood straight as a gun barrel.

"We don't have time for this, Twister," warned Turrety Knocks.

Hack wrinkled his nose as if he'd smelled something yucky. "Is that so? Do you have time for this?" He launched himself forward and punched Turrety Knocks, who crumpled to the ground.

"Take a hold of his legs," said Hack.

"I ain't doing nothing to help you," I spat.

I daren't bring Wah out of my pocket. If Hack clapped eyes on it he'd know it was something precious and steal it. And I would not risk losing the necklace again.

I looked around. Maybe I could make a run for it and raise the alarm? I shot a glance at Hack. That was when I spotted the knife sticking out from the side of his boot.

"Used to work at the old slaughterhouse in Sungrave. Learned how to put a bull out of its misery real quick. Butchering it was harder, mind. Took real upper arm strength. But once you learned where to make the right cuts it was easy. Could have done it in my sleep." Hack smiled. "Do as I say and there'll be no need for me to use it on your friend." He patted the knife and then rolled his trouser leg back down.

I knew he meant it. Hack ain't been in prison for stealing candy. Perhaps if I did as I was told, I could buy some time to figure out another way to stop him.

Hack and I lifted Turrety Knocks up and shuffled across the yard to the barn. I scanned the fields but nobody was around. I checked the road too: if there was dust flying up on it, it meant a truck was coming. But I couldn't see nothing.

We stepped inside the barn. My guts squirmed. I

sensed something bad was going to happen. We took Turrety Knocks over to a pile of rolled-up wire fencing.

I spied a spade by the straw bales.

We placed Turrety Knocks on the ground, Hack grunting as he hoisted the old man up into a sitting position.

Quick as wings, I lunged to grab the spade. I raised it above my head and brought it down hard as I could, catching Hack on the shoulder. He cried out and lost his balance. I brought the spade back up and swung it towards his head, but Hack sprang at me, knocking me flat on my back. The spade flew out of my hand and struck the ground. Hack pinned me down and slapped me hard. My ears rang.

"Try that again and his throat's as good as cut," he said, dragging me over to Turrety Knocks. Hack lashed some old rope round and round and round us. Turrety Knocks slumped forward. Hack finished tying the knot and hurried out the barn.

"Turrety Knocks!" I whispered. "You hear me?"

Nothing. He was out cold.

Hack returned with a red container. He unscrewed the lid and poured its contents over the straw bales.

A sharp, clawing smell hit my nostrils. I could taste it at the back of my throat. It nipped my eyes.

It was gasoline.

Hack splashed some more around the barn and tossed the container behind the bales. The blue lady on Hack's arm shone with sweat. Hack wiped her across his brow.

He walked over to us. "I warned you to stay away from Clem. That's twice you've made him look like a gutless sissy. Every boy from here to Pineville is going to think they can knock him around senseless and I ain't having that. This here's a clear message I'm sending – if you mess with my boy, you've got me to deal with."

I did not know my heart could beat so fast.

Hack shoved his hand into his pocket and brought out a matchbox. He took a match out and struck it. It spluttered and hissed and flared.

"Two against one ain't a fair fight, Firecracker. I ain't playing fair neither."

"No!" I shouted.

Hack dropped the match and strode towards the door. He slammed it shut behind him.

A line of flame shot towards me and Turrety Knocks.

My ears filled with the crackling of straw and wood and sacks catching fire. The floor moved with mice fleeing the flames.

I tried to stand but Turrety Knocks weighed me down. I rocked from side to side in an attempt to loosen the rope, but it only cut deeper into my flesh.

"Turrety Knocks!" I yelled. "Wake up!"

He didn't move. He was somewhere I couldn't bring him back from.

Thick smoke curled up like black snakes ready to strike.

I coughed. The heat and fumes made it hard to breathe. I had to do something otherwise we'd be roasted like a couple of hogs at a barn dance.

If I could reach Wah, I might be able to put the fire out. I concentrated hard trying to get my hand into my pocket, but it was no good. My arms were tied tightly to my sides.

My lungs heaved up and down and up and down.

I thought 'bout Point and his red squeaky ball and the way he'd nudge me with his nose when he sensed I was sad. But then I remembered him lying on the barn floor with the rusty knife in his chest.

Tears streaked down my face. Aunt Honey said sometimes people get so sad they cry rivers. I wished I could cry one now to put the fire out.

Aunt Honey. If she'd been here, she would have known what to do. She always knew what to do. And she always knew the right thing to say too. If I was ever upset or angry, her words made me feel better again.

Wah tingled in my pocket. I felt a jolt of electricity travel through my body. I must have got it wrong! I didn't have to be wearing Wah around my neck for the magic to happen after all!

My heart started to grow.

I thought 'bout Aunt Honey again. She had always been there for me through thin and thick. I thought 'bout her chewing fast and laughing hard and gossiping 'bout the folks in Culleroy.

My heart swelled up huge. The cracking of the lickety-flames faded away. I croaked, "Thank you for putting the fire out."

I thought I heard a thousand voices chanting. Though it could have been the mice squeaking. I wasn't sure if it was the heat or not, but the necklace glowed pink-hot.

I could see some soul in the air!

Mice and spiders and beetles whizzed straight past me. A big swirl of orange bubbles filled with dancing flames rose up from the floor. Fire must have a soul too! That was when it struck me – all the bubbles I could see hadn't blown in from the four corners of the globe; they were coming from what was trapped inside the barn.

How could the soul of a bat or an owl stop a raging fire?

I heard an almighty smash. I looked up. The window had broken! For a split-moment, I seen a large yellow ball of light beside it. It looked mighty similar to the one I seen in Holler Woods that had lead me to Maymay's. But it was hard to tell for sure.

Fresh air tumbled in, chasing the choking smoke away. The fire leapt up twice as high. It was angry and hungry and crept ever nearer. My skin started to tighten.

A bubble appeared through the smoke. There was a tree inside it! It drifted over to the burning food sacks and burst. The fire must be destroying the souls!

Just as my heart was sinking, a green bubble flew past a wooden beam, zoomed towards me and disappeared straight into my pocket. Wah must have swallowed it 'cause all of a sudden I smelled soil and fizzy-fruit and warm flowers and rotting leaves and mossy-stone and brown rivers and mud and stagnant puddles.

Pain jabbed at my muscles and my bones creaked.

I lifted my head up.

My body was fast turning into a mass of green foliage!

The necklace must have taken the wrong soul. *How could a bunch of leaves put a raging fire out?*

I was agile.

Nimble.

Supple.

I slipped through the rope and moved in all different directions at the same time.

I held treasures and riches and cures. They were deep, dark secrets locked within me, waiting to be discovered. Folks thought I was savage and scary and poisonous and death. But really, I was life itself.

My vines and creepers snaked along the floor. I dodged the flames and wound myself around tool handles and over leather saddles and under log piles. I even curled around Turrety Knocks, pulling him away from the flames.

Up.

Up.

Up.

I climbed towards the light. Every part of me was bursting with energy.

The fire roared below, but there were other sounds too. Toucans shrieked and monkeys whooped and mosquitoes whined and leopards snarled and frogs peeped and giant bees hummed.

I reached the window.

The air was thick and damp and heavy and misty. My leaves shivered.

Rain started to fall.

I was no ordinary forest. I was a rainforest.

The raindrops turned into a torrent of water.

Steam rose, thick and billowing. A last gasp from the fire below.

Anacondas uncurled and piranhas snapped and jaguars pounced and a caiman blinked. Ripe fruit dropped and stinky flowers opened and an ocelot hissed and a sloth didn't move not one muscle.

When the fire had all but disappeared, I wobbled and swayed. I crashed down from high above.

I lifted my head.

Nothing was broken. But it sure felt as if everything had broken. I spat grit from my mouth. That hurt too.

The barn stood scorched and smouldering. I smelled buckled metal and melted plastic and burnt earth and white ash and smouldering sacks and hot mice and storm puddles.

All the vines and trees and critters and lightning and rain had vanished.

Turrety Knocks lay by the wall. I crawled over to him. He sure was like a cat with eleven lives. His eyes were closed but I could hear him breathing. The smoke had turned his face black and his wrinkles white.

I found his hanky. Thought it best to clean him up a little. As I opened it some things fallen out: fishing wire and two bottle tops and a dead weevil and tobaccy and a photograph. I picked it up. It was soft and cracked and faint. As if it had been held a thousand times or more. Turrety Knocks was in it. But it was like another Turrety Knocks 'cause there were fewer worry lines on his face. And sadness hadn't fogged up his eyes neither, they were twinkling. His hair was neatly combed and he was standing proud. I can't say I'd ever seen Turrety Knocks looking so happy. His arm was around a pretty lady who was smiling. Must have been his wife, Bethy. Bang-slap between them was a girl who'd long hair and dark eyes and a white frilly dress on.

I gasped.

It was Beam! *But how could that be?*

Beam and Lula must be the same person! But hadn't Lula been killed in a fire?

I let go of the photo. It fluttered to the ground.

Maymay told me ghosts were real.

Fast as three-lined lizards chasing ants, it all started

to make sense. Beam had wanted me to look out for Turrety Knocks 'cause he was her pa! Of course! She'd been at Point's funeral but nobody had asked me who she was. That's 'cause they couldn't see her. And no wonder she'd been so angry 'bout me taking Wah. She'd lost her life 'cause of the necklace and White Eye.

My Beam was a ghost!

But why had she kept this from me? That's when I remembered her words. *Best friends tell each other 99.9% everything.*

Turrety Knocks murmured. He opened an eye. "Twister?" he rasped.

I hooked my arm under his and hauled him up.

"Thank you," Turrety Knocks whispered.

"I'll fetch help," I said.

His hand touched my arm. "Someone will be here soon enough 'cause of the smoke," he said. "Did you use the necklace to put the fire out?"

I nodded.

"You've got some leaves on you," he said.

I brushed them off my arms. I shook my head for good measure too. A hummingbird shot out and hovered in the air before darting off towards the roof.

"I'll get you some water," I said, yanking some stubborn ivy off my legs.

"Twister, that's the second time you've used the necklace here. White Eye will be coming for you."

The barn door fallen off its hinges and slammed on to the ground, making the pair of us jump.

I groaned. I was cat-tired and achy-sore and scared-stiff.

Turrety Knocks's blackened skin made his moss and bark eyes lighter. "You told me Maymay didn't force you, so why did you take the necklace?" he asked.

"I want Pa back home 'cause everything's better when he's around."

"Then you'd best go now, while you've still got the chance," said Turrety Knocks.

"What'll you say to Ma and Aunt Honey? They'll be here soon with Doc."

"That you managed to escape from Hack and I told you to hide somewhere safe."

"If I see White Eye ... and it don't go to plan." I stopped. "Will you look after Ma and ..."

Turrety Knocks interrupted me. "Twister, you've saved my life twice now. Whatever it is you have to do, you can do it. There's no doubt 'bout it." He smiled at me. He meant what he said too. I seen it in his eyes.

"There's something I have to tell you," I said.

Turrety Knocks frowned.

"I'm certain I seen a big ball of light by the window on the roof. Whatever it was smashed the glass so air could get in. Without it, I couldn't have put the fire out."

Turrety Knocks's eyebrows rose.

"It ain't the first time I've come across this light neither. It guided me to Maymay's cabin when I got lost in Holler Woods." I stopped to take a deep breath. "I met a girl by Juniper Falls that same night. She'd dark eyes and long hair and wore a white dress. She's funny and smart and caring and kind. She's the bestest friend you could ever wish for." I picked the picture up from the ground. I blew some ash off it. "The girl I'm talking 'bout is the same one that's in this photo. She told me her name was Beam and she's been helping me all along. I think you should know she loves you with all her heart."

Turrety Knocks took the photo from my hands. His face lit up looking at it.

"I called her Beam 'cause she was the happiest soul I'd ever met," he said. "I ain't seen her myself, but I sense her around me all the time and take great comfort from it." Turrety Knocks's moss and bark eyes glistened. They shone the same as they had done in the creased and faded photo.

I felt ten out of ten, prize-winning jittery at the top of Black Smoke Hill. The air was thick and heavy. If a bush rustled or a branch cracked or a blackbird gave a warning cry – I'd stand still as fence posts. White Eye had to be close. He might even be watching me right now.

Wah gleamed in the sunlight. When I touched the necklace, all my nerves fidgeted and twitched. My energy returned as if I'd been plugged into an invisible electric socket. Every ache in my body vanished.

I closed my eyes and I thought 'bout Pa. I pictured his smile and the dimples in his cheeks. The time had come to find out where he was.

My heart stretched and grew with each thump.

"Thank you for taking me to Pa," I said.

The wind hushed. Trees leant in and ants froze on the path. Even the buzzy-flies stopped cleaning their wings.

Wah felt hot against my skin. I thought I heard a thousand voices chanting. Though it could have been the noises of the forest rising up from the valley below.

My eyes widened.

Millions of soul bubbles were flying over Culleroy.

A brown bubble zoomed fast as rockets into Wah's copper mouth. I felt as if someone had wrapped a wet blanket around me. Pain torn through my body. My bones cracked. I cried out and fallen over.

Every inch of me was covered in thick, glossy feathers. I stood up. I had a long brown feather tail and yellow talons for feet. I looked mighty similar to Pa's favourite bird – the golden eagle.

I hopped towards the edge of the hill and opened my wings. Without even thinking 'bout it, I jumped over the side.

I tumbled forward, striking leaves and smacking off branches. In a panic, I flapped my arms like crazy-mad.

I rose up.

Up.

Up.

I could fly!

This was the best feeling *ever*.

I was lighter.

And sharp-eyed. I spied mice quivering and shrews

shuddering and songbirds quaking and hares zigzagging and foxes trembling.

I was a hunter. Nothing escaped my claws.

The wind was my friend. The warm breeze carried me. If I straightened my wings, I could glide, smooth and steady. And if I lifted a wing tip, I could turn in a circle and drop down.

The land underneath me whizzed by. It was laid out like a green and brown and gold and red and yellow patchwork quilt. A giant silver worm wriggled its way across it. It was Raging River!

Aunt Honey said the sky must be full of voices on account of the fact that folks always talked to the heavens when they were praying. But I didn't hear no muttering or pleading or cussing. Only the breeze whistling past and the call of Raging River and the whispering trees. There was a peace up here you couldn't find on the ground.

I circled and dived down towards Holler Woods. My wings brushed the branches as I flapped through the trees. I glided into the clearing at Juniper Falls and headed for the white wall of tumbling water.

I stuck my feet out and spread my tail feathers to slow

myself down. I did not want to smack into the cliff face behind it.

Too late!

I braced myself. The shock of the cold water took my breath away. I shot straight through the waterfall and out the other side.

I landed hard, hitting rock. Everything spun round and round and round and turned to black.

Lying face down on cold stone wasn't so comfortable. I sat up. If Ma and Aunt Honey could see me now they'd give me away to the travelling circus for sure. Some brown feathers were sticking out of my arms and legs. I plucked them out one by one.

I glanced around. I was in a cave, with a waterfall hurrying past the entrance. Somewhere, further into the gloom, I heard a high-pitched drip-sploosh noise.

I shook the fog from my brain. My body was a whole mass of angry nerve endings. I wobbled and stumbled forward.

I could smell the dark. And glistening rock and algae and bats and glow-worms and spiders' webs and smoke and fungus. But I couldn't smell Pa.

He just had to be here.

"Pa? It's me, Twister."

Silence. Except for the waterfall and the drip-sploosh of water.

"I've come to fetch you home. Ma's not been well. Aunt Honey and me are trying our best but I think you're the only one who can make her better again." My voice grew small. "We lost Point too. We miss you so much."

The necklace throbbed freezy-cold. Must have been 'cause it got wet passing through the water.

Pa had to be alive, otherwise why would Wah have brought me here? But what if he didn't want to be found?

I took another step forward. My head smacked off something cold and hard. Pain travelled through my skull. A large rock icicle hung down from the ceiling. I would be no use to anyone if I knocked myself out. When my eyes stopped seeing stars, I moved again.

Up ahead, I spied pretty shafts of sunlight coming down from a hole in the roof of the cave, illuminating a circle of rocks on the cave floor. There was a pile of charred wood in the middle of them. Someone had had a merry fire crackling. I edged my way forward, careful not to slip or trip or bash my head.

By the side of the stones lay a piece of clothing. Could that be Pa's? I picked up something soft and woollen and full of holes.

Why! It was Maymay's violet shawl! What on earth was it doing in the cave? Had she known the whole time that Pa was here and not told me?

Wah was so cold I thought it'd near burn my skin.

All of a sudden, the waterfall sounded different, almost as though it had stopped falling. I ducked behind a pile of rocks. Cautiously, I peeped out from behind them. A figure walked through the water and stepped into the cave.

My heart leapt with joy. Was that Pa?

I couldn't quite see his face. His hair wasn't white; it was long and dark. Perhaps that was 'cause it was wet. His clothes were black and torn, as if he'd travelled through a hundred storms to get here. In his hand, he held a gnarled stick and a sack was slung over his shoulder. It moved and twitched. Something was inside it that wasn't too happy 'bout being inside it.

I lifted Wah away from my skin 'cause it hurt so bad. The copper was as cold as frost. Wah had never been as uncomfortable as that before.

Fast as flying arrows, I remembered Maymay's warning 'bout Wah turning cold.

It wasn't Pa who was in here with me.

It was White Eye!

My heart hammered in my ears. I steadied myself, careful not to make a sound.

White Eye chucked the wriggling sack on the floor and propped his stick against the wall. He walked over to a spindly tree. A long coat hung off one of its branches. It was made from matted fur and wolf claws and rabbit tails and beaks and fish bones and pigs' ears and stink bugs and red centipedes and girls' pigtails and faded snakeskin and black feathers and stinging plants and razor-sharp thorns. It was alive too 'cause there was things crawly-creeping all over it.

White Eye took the coat down and put it on.

It made a loud clinking noise.

White Eye reached inside it and brought out a small blue bottle. He crouched down and placed it on the ground. He untied the rope around the sack and pulled out a flapping crow. It cawed and pecked at him. He tightened his grip around its neck. It gasped.

I knew exactly what White Eye was going to do. He

was 'bout to kill the crow so he could steal its soul! No way could I sit and watch that happen.

"You leave the poor crow be! You hear me?" I yelled.

White Eye shot to his feet. The crow freed itself and flew to safety.

I heard the same cracking noise a tree makes after someone shouts "*Timber!*". It came from the stick. Two large yellow eyes appeared in the wood. They blinked.

A mouth broke open. It was full of long, sharp, jagged, splintery teeth. To my astonishment, it spoke.

"Twig says: Holler Woods be empty; lakes and mountains clear. Worry not, White Eye, for the necklace and the girl be here."

I fled to the back of the cave, scrabbling my way around the slimy rock, desperate to find a hole big enough for me to escape through. My nostrils filled with the smell of damp cellars and rotting sacks and decaying leather and stale spit and sour meat. I turned around: right behind me stood White Eye. My legs buckled as if my bones were made from marshmallow. He grabbed a hold of my T-shirt and dragged me to the front of the cave. The rock stole the skin from my knees.

White Eye hoisted me on to my feet. His lips opened in a smile. One of his eyes was the colour of the bottom of the ocean. The other was as white as bones. He stared deep into my soul.

I was too scared to blink.

White Eye shifted his gaze to the one thing he wanted more than anything else. He brought his hand up to touch Wah. The necklace warmed around my neck. White Eye traced his fingers over the copper face. Wah's mouth snapped opened, showing rows of shiny teeth. They bit down on one of White Eye's fingers. He leapt back, yanking his hand away, but the tip of his finger was missing. Black worms wriggled out from the wound. White Eye snarled. It sounded as if he'd beasts trapped in his belly.

A cracking sound filled the cave. The stick laughed. Clouds of sawdust puffed out from his mouth.

"Twig says: Patience, White Eye! The time is not right. Remember the necklace must be taken without a fight."

Anger flooded every vein in my body. White Eye hadn't won yet. I still had Wah, and I wasn't giving up on finding Pa neither. He must be somewhere in this cave.

My heart grew bigger and stronger with each beat, swelling up fierce.

The waterfall gave me an idea.

I closed my eyes and whispered some words under my breath.

I thought I heard a thousand voices chanting.

Bubbles began to appear. Lots of them were filled with teeny-tiny noisy waterfalls. A whole load of green moss and rock bubbles floated near the hole in the roof. A black scorpion curled its tail as it rolled past me.

White Eye picked up the rope from the sack, moving behind me to tie my hands together. A blue glowing bubble flashed across the cave straight into Wah's mouth, travelling speedier than a hare running from a fox.

Everything quietened except for whistles and clicks in my ears, the same noises I heard when I put my head under the water in the bath. Hurt flowed through my body from the tips of my hair to the ends of my toes, but I tried my best not to cry out.

I swear the cave rippled in front of my eyes. The clumsiness of my bones and body vanished.

I was small.

Light shone through me.

I was fluid.

I slipped through White Eye's fingers and raced

towards the ground. White Eye roared. I splashed on to the cave floor and trickled in to Juniper Falls.

I was no longer a single drop of water.

I was a whole rushing, whooshing, tumbling river.

I was mighty.

I pounded rock into sand and carried ships and carved my way through mountains.

Down.

Down.

Down, I fallen.

No rollercoaster ride at the fairground could beat this.

When I hit the pool, I fizzed so much it made me hoot! I whooshed round and round and round. With each swirl I grew bigger, until I became the whole pool.

The wind blew soothing patterns on my surface. Pond skaters and water-spiders and boatmen tippy-toed softly across me. Duckweeds swayed and hornweed blushed red. Fish wiggled and flicked and jumped. Dragonflies skimmed and beetles dived and nymphs hatched and damselflies pulsed and water fleas danced. Lily pads closed softly and birds fluttered and bathed, and deer sipped. All the roots of the trees and the plants slowly drawn me into them and pulled me towards the heavens.

When the moon and stars touched me, I shivered with delight. Every bit of me rippled and sparkled with the sweet joy of it.

A hand slapped my face. It sure done sting some.

Water gushed from my mouth. I coughed my guts up and gasped for breath. I think I'd just swallowed the whole pool, and a couple of minnows for good measure.

My body was a whole world of pain.

"Found you floating face down," said a gruff voice. "I thought White Eye had got you and stolen your soul."

I was lying on the grass by Juniper Falls. Night had arrived. Everything was as dark as molasses, but I'd recognize that voice anywhere.

"I managed to escape," I croaked.

Maymay sat in the shadows. From what I could make out, she looked like she'd been dragged through a hedge forward. Even the other witches in Holler Woods would have got a fright if they'd seen her.

Water streamed out of my eyes and my nose and my ears.

"You took the soul of Juniper Falls. Clever," said

Maymay. I think she meant it as a compliment, but the way she said it, she sounded more annoyed.

I coughed and spluttered, wiping the water from my face. "Have you seen White Eye?" I asked, glancing all around.

"No, but he'll be hunting for you, so we need to leave," said Maymay.

The necklace nipped at my skin. "I think he's close, Wah's growing colder."

"Can you stand?"

There wasn't half an ounce of energy left in me.

Not waiting for my reply, she hoisted me up on to my feet. Boy, she must have eaten all her oats that morning 'cause she was awful strong for a lady of her advanced years.

"Beam told me you'd left," I said.

"I can't very well protect you from White Eye if I'm not here, can I?"

Maymay had been around the whole time keeping an eye on me! Aunt Honey said there were hidden depths in every person. I guess she was right.

"Twister, we're wasting time with idle chit-chat," she said.

I hesitated. "Maymay, I need to go back into the cave before White Eye gets here. I just know Pa's in there."

"It's far too risky. Your pa wouldn't want you to get yourself killed."

"But this could be my last chance," I said.

"I should never have allowed you to take Wah," said Maymay.

It hurt when I raised my eyebrows. "You said the necklace chose me!"

"I did? I must have been mistaken."

"Mistaken? Mistaken! You went on and on 'bout it!"

"It's wise to remember everyone makes mistakes. It's what makes us human. Listen to me; I'll cast another spell to make sure the necklace stays hidden. We'll leave town for a while, until White Eye realizes the trail has gone cold. He'll eventually have to return to wherever he came from. It might not work, but it's the only way I can think of saving your life, Twister."

"What 'bout Pa?"

"When I hide the necklace, you'll not be able to use its magic again. It's far too dangerous. You'll need to find him by another means."

"I asked Wah to show me where Pa is – and I ended up in White Eye's cave. He wasn't there though."

Maymay thought 'bout this. "The necklace took you to the cave for a reason; you clearly don't have the brains to work it out. Wah is wasted on you."

Her mood was blacker than cellars. I gave Maymay a hard stare. She'd changed her tune. I needed to explore the cave one last time, but the necklace was so cold it was near sticking to my skin. "If we left, where would we go?" I asked.

"I've friends who can keep us safe in Tarnoma."

"That's a trillion miles away," I said. I thought 'bout Ma and Aunt Honey and Beam and Turrety Knocks. A lump near blocked my throat. Leaving them would be mighty hard. But the thought of never finding Pa was way too much to bear. Especially after everything that had happened. Today hadn't worked out as planned, but if I quit now, it'd be like throwing the trowel in. Or something like that.

"Maymay, Pa's in that cave. I promise you can have the necklace as soon as I've spoken to him."

"You're more foolish than I thought. Give the necklace to me and you'll walk away from this alive. Otherwise your stubbornness will be the end of you."

"I realize this, but I've made my decision. There's nothing you can say to change my mind," I said in a none-too-friendly way, sticking my chin out for good measure.

"Give me Wah!" she hissed.

"No, Maymay! I won't. Wah ain't yours to take. I'm its owner now. Why, you're as slippery as bathtubs. One minute you're my friend and the next you ain't. I know you're up to something 'cause I seen your shawl in the cave. And as for Pa, I'll find him with or without your help."

"No wonder he left," she spat, "with such a useless and selfish daughter. Go ahead and get yourself killed. See if I care."

It was as though Maymay had slapped me again. My cheeks flushed and my eyes blurred and my heart shrank. I'd never heard her *this* mean before.

I was 'bout to shove past her, when I stopped. My guts niggled at me some.

"Answer me this and I'll give you Wah. What was my dog called?" I said.

Maymay spoke through gritted teeth. "You want to talk 'bout your dog when White Eye could show up any second now?"

"I do."

"I'm hopeless with names."

"You definitely know it."

"In case it's escaped your attention, I'm an old lady, and old ladies can be forgetful."

"Ask your spirit guides then."

"They're busy," snapped Maymay, glaring at me. She sighed and muttered under her breath. "Is it Buddy?"

"Wrong!"

"Patch?"

"Nope. One more guess."

"This is *impossible*," she said. "Wolfie?"

I blinked.

My jaw dropped open.

I stepped back from her.

The noise of Juniper Falls thundered around us.

She really wasn't Maymay! The real Maymay had said to be careful 'cause White Eye could take the form of whatever or whoever he wanted. She said he'd try to trick me into giving the necklace to him.

It was White Eye! He'd stolen Maymay's soul and that's why her shawl had been in the cave!

Maymay stormed out of the shadows into the moonlight. Her green eye with the black tear mark on it gleamed in the silvery light. Her other eye was as white as ghosts.

"Stay away from me!" I shouted.

Maymay swayed from side to side. As if being pulled and pushed by invisible hands. Something rippled under her skin. It split open and fallen away like it was paper. Much the same as a cocoon done when a butterfly emerged from it. Except it ain't no butterfly. It was White Eye and Twig.

There was a crunching noise as Twig's yellow eyes appeared. He re-cracked his mouth open and bared his splintery teeth.

"Twig says: Twister, Twister, how clever you've been. But here comes something you never could have foreseen."

White Eye raised his arm and brought Twig down across the side of my head. I swear beautiful fireflies danced in the air before the darkness came for me.

A thudding noise woke me. My skull throbbed and my nose itched and my ears rang.

I heard the noise again. Was it the sound of the pain in my head? Or something else?

What was left of Maymay lay next to me on the grass. I swallowed back the tears. I never right knew if I could trust her – but I sure as heck would miss her. I'd never felt so alone.

All I wanted was Ma to wrap her arms around me and tell me everything would be all right. Like she used to 'cause there was no safer place in the world to be than that. But I had more pressing things to do. I had to stop White Eye from getting Wah.

I peered through the gloom. It was White Eye who was making the racket. He was hammering Twig into the ground with a rock. When Twig had all but disappeared, White Eye reached into his coat. He brought out a folded-up leaf. Inside it was a green powder, which he poured over Twig. A red mist appeared and swirled around them until the wind moved it on.

The ground rumbled. Twig whined. A huge black tree rose up from the forest floor. Earth rained down all around me.

Twig pushed and twisted up.

Up.

Up.

Until with one last crack, he shuddered to a halt. It was as if Twig had been in Holler Woods for hundreds of years. Except there wasn't no names or love hearts carved into his trunk.

The other trees in the clearing were shocked 'cause they held their breaths.

Twig's roots rudely felt their way through the soil beneath me, and my body bumped up and down and up and down.

I heard loud tearing noises. Branches snaked out of Twig's trunk. They felt their way over the stars and scratched the face of the moon. As soon as they'd filled the sky above me, buds popped open and leaves appeared. They were light green and shiny and whispering. My ears then filled with a dry crackling sound. The leaves turned danger-danger red and withered. The tree trunk groaned as it shook itself. Every single leaf dropped off its branches, covering the forest floor in a crunchy crimson carpet. Lichen sprouted from the bare branches. The bark on its trunk split and deep lines formed like wrinkles. And right in front of my eyes, the tree turned white as maggots.

A hand grabbed me. My heart leapt into my mouth. I'd been so busy gawping at Twig, I'd forgotten to watch out for White Eye.

He dragged me over to the tree, the tips of my boots ploughing lines in the grass.

Two huge eyes appeared on the tree trunk. Twig turned from side to side and leant back. With an almighty crack, a huge mouth appeared. Green sap dripped from the sides of it. It was as dark as closed coffins inside.

White Eye shoved me closer. Twig's breath blasted us

as he spoke. I smelled sour apple and stagnant water and old hog bones and coal tar and yellow cabbage and mushy cucumber.

"Twig says: Twister, the time has come for the necklace to be taken. Enter the place where the living are forsaken."

"No!" I yelled. White Eye pushed me so hard, I fallen straight into Twig's gaping jaws.

It was dark and hot and slippy and drippy and prickly. There were splinters sticking out from everywhere and hundreds of pink eyes glowed in the dark. I wasn't sure what they belonged to, but if you got too close to them they hissed. Bones were scattered everywhere.

I could hear Twig's breathing in my ears. Almost as if I was walking through the depths of his guts. Ma always said a stroll was good for lifting the spirits, but in here, my heart was sinking with every step. Just knowing White Eye was behind me made me weak at the ankles.

Happens Maymay was right: I didn't stand a chance against him. The necklace stopped tingling the split-moment I entered Twig's mouth. It just pinched at my skin with its iciness.

She'd warned that White Eye would take me to a place where there weren't any living souls. But where could that be?

I spied a teeny-tiny circle of light glowing in the distance. The light grew and grew until it blinded me. White Eye gave me one last almighty shove and I flew out of the tree and landed on some grass.

White Eye jumped down from Twig's open mouth.

I glanced around. Were we back where we started? I was still in Holler Woods. Night-time had vanished; the sun shone in the sky. I seen the trees and the bushes and the flowers and Juniper Falls. And the ants and the crickets and the bees and the crows and the buzzy-flies.

But something wasn't right. I couldn't smell the scorched grass or sweet flowers or fiery sun or baked earth or wilted herbs or yellow pollen or molten pine sap. Or the leaves and the clouds and the breath of Juniper Falls. It was as if they were alive, but lifeless.

Where was I?

The noise of breaking wood filled the air.

"Twig says: Welcome, Twister – to your new home. This is the spirit plane – where the dead roam."

I shook. I didn't belong here. I figured the only way back to the real Holler Woods would be through Twig. But how would I ever get past those horrible teeth?

I whispered urgently to the necklace, "Thank you, Wah, for helping me back to the farm." But it stayed cold as mountain peaks.

Twig laughed. Sawdust filled the air.

"Twig says: Oh, Twister! The necklace is of no use to you here. This means it's the end of the road for you, my dear."

My heart missed some beats. The world spun and my breath was fast and shallow.

White Eye reached into his rotten, writhing coat. He brought out a small purple glass bottle. He uncorked it and greedily drank its contents, then took off his coat and hung it on one of Twig's branches.

Twig cackled. It sounded the same as thousands of sticks hitting off each other.

"Twig says: I hate to say goodbye, for this has been so much fun. White Eye's going to change now; it's time for you to run."

Change? What had been in the bottle?

All of a sudden, he collapsed on the ground. Long

claws popped out from his fingertips, fur sprouted from his face and his teeth grew whiter and longer.

I ran fast as a bullet out a gun towards the trees.

White Eye snarled somewhere behind me.

Holler Woods was one big green smear. Branches scraped my face and roots made me stumble. Sweat trickled into my eyes, blinding me.

I couldn't think. My head was broken with fear.

I shot into a clearing and stopped. My chest heaved up and down and up and down. Which way should I go?

White Eye crashed through the undergrowth after me. Then it went quiet.

I sensed I was being watched.

There, at the edge of the trees, a large black cat sniffed at the ground. One of its eyes was olive-coloured. The other was white. White Eye must have taken the soul of a panther! It lifted its head and snarled, then padded across the clearing towards me. I scanned the ground for a stick or a rock to arm myself with. I couldn't see nothing. Besides, something told me it ain't smart taking your eyes off a big, hissy cat for a split-moment.

Some bushes shook next to the panther. It halted. The

leaves rustled again. The panther flicked its tail. Out of the bushes flew Point, barking ferociously.

My heart sang.

I yelled, "Careful, Point!"

He ran in circles around the panther, which lashed out with its mighty front paws. Point merrily taunted it by bouncing around and yipping. Surely but slowly, he drew it away from me.

"Twistie!" shouted a voice. "Over here!"

My head snapped round. All I could see were trees.

"Now would be a good time to get moving!"

I spied two legs swinging forwards and backwards from a giant oak tree. I only knew one person who'd climb a tree in a frilly dress like that.

I heard the long low rumble of a deep belly growl behind me.

"Twistie, keep on walking. Don't look behind you," she yelled.

The panther roared.

"R-U-N!" Beam screeched.

Every nerve in my body woke up. I sprinted the last few steps and leapt up as high as I could on to the tree trunk. The bark was old and worn and shiny and it was hard for my boots to get a grip. I dug my heels and nails right in, reaching out to grasp a hold of a sturdy branch. I heaved myself on to it as the panther paced beneath showing me its rippy-flesh teeth.

I lost my balance and slipped, dangling in the air like bait on a fishing hook. The panther flattened its ears and hurled itself up at me. Just as I was sure it would sink its claws into my leg, two arms stretched down and hauled me up to safety.

Beam hugged me. All light as feathers and cold as coins. She grinned. The three moles on her face wrinkled up. I don't think I'd ever been so pleased to see her.

"This sure beats trying to catch green fish," she said, puffing the hair out of her eyes.

"Would now be a good time to tell you that I've missed you?"

"Seeing as how we're stuck here, I'm all ears," said Beam.

"What I said to you in the barn was not 'cause I didn't like you. I thought if you kept away from me, you'd be safe from White Eye. I was trying to protect you is all."

"How's that working out for you? Keeping me out of harm's way?" she asked.

"Not so well." I shrugged, glancing down at the panther, which had begun to climb the tree. "Especially seeing as I needn't have worried 'bout White Eye killing you 'cause you're already dead."

"Oh, he could banish my soul for ever from the spirit plane if he wanted to, but I take your point. I never told you I was a ghostie."

"I'm so sorry for what White Eye done to you and your ma, Beam."

For a split-moment Beam faded in front of my eyes.

"Why didn't you say something?" I said. "Was it 'cause of the 0.01% that best friends don't tell each other?"

Beam wrung her hands together. "Not everyone can see me, but those who can are terrified of me. I was scared to tell you the truth 'cause I thought you might not want nothing more to do with me. It ain't exactly normal being a ghostie, you know."

"Well, you can be frightening at times. Especially with that temper of yours."

Beam whacked me on the arm.

"I never knew you could see a ghost in the daytime," I said.

"That's me; always full of surprises."

"And to think I told you to put a vest on 'cause you were cold."

The panther was way better at climbing trees than me. The branches beneath us trembled.

"Beam?"

"Yes, Twistie?"

"That ain't a panther. It's White Eye. He stole Maymay's soul and I think he's planning on taking mine too. The necklace can't save me here."

"Not what I was wanting to hear," she said. "Any thoughts on what we should do next?"

The panther clawed its way up the trunk until it was level with us. With an almighty leap, it landed on the branch we were perched on. Beam and I shuffled away from it and the branch grumbled and sloped downwards at a sharp angle.

"You're way better at saving my own skin than I am," I said.

Beam gulped. "Except this time, I'm fresh out of ideas."

With an almighty shudder, the branch snapped in two.

Down.

Down.

Down Beam and me and the panther all fallen.

I landed hard. Every breath in me was knocked out of me. Beam was lying, unmoving, next to me, eyes closed.

The panther wobbled to its feet. Before I could cry out, it pounced on Beam. Her eyes opened wide. I crawled on to my knees. The black cat jumped and struck me with its giant paw, the force of it knocking me on to the ground. The panther turned back to Beam, opening its jaws.

"No!" I cried.

Rays of light shone out from Beam's body. They were so bright I couldn't see her no more. She vanished in a flash. Hundreds of teeny-tiny yellow bubbles floated up from where she'd been lying into the tree above, each one as glorious as the sun. All the tree's leaves glowed golden.

I didn't flinch when the panther's two paws hit my chest. The weight of it squeezed the last drops of air from my lungs. I watched the lights fading in the tree. If I kept still, it would be over quick. Maybe if I turned into soul bubbles too, I could be with Beam and Point again.

I felt weightless. Like I'd drunk ten pots of Silver Cloudtip tea. Everything became quiet, even my heart. As I slipped into a dream, the panther hissed. It leapt off me and backed away, pawing at itself.

Air found its way into my aching lungs. I gasped for breath, like a fish stranded on a riverbank. White Eye's teeth and claws and fur and rage vanished. He'd changed back into himself! He staggered to his feet and lurched towards me with his arms outstretched.

I couldn't move. Tears streamed down my cheeks.

White Eye dropped to my side. He took the necklace from me and held it up. Wah's copper face was frozen in a scream. White Eye looked at me as his hands closed around my neck. I stared into his cold moon of an eye.

Something caught his attention and his gaze shifted.

A boy was standing next to us. Before I could blink, the child whooshed into White Eye's body.

A lady who looked exactly like Beam's ma, Bethy, stepped forwards. White Eye let go of me, struggling to get up. She smiled at me before rushing towards him. He tried to push her away, but she passed straight through his flailing arms and vanished into his chest. White Eye's skin bulged and rippled, as if things were moving underneath it.

A crowd of men, women and children appeared. One by one, they flashed into White Eye's writhing body. He stumbled backwards, muttering some words, his eyes wide. A red mist swirled up from the ground. It wrapped itself around White Eye, protecting him. I gasped when the mist turned into a wall of heads. One of the heads snaked out on a long red neck towards a young girl. Its jaws opening up wide, until it looked as though it could swallow her whole. The girl froze, too petrified to run.

"You leave her be!" I shouted.

All the heads swivelled to watch me stand, their black eyes gleaming.

I gritted my teeth. White Eye had taken my Beam from me and he'd destroyed Turrety Knocks's family.

If he thought he was going to steal my soul and kill the children of Culleroy, then he had another thing coming.

The rage coursing through my veins woke up every cell in my body.

"Don't you know it's rude to stare?" I said.

The head zoomed over to me.

My fist flew out to punch it on the nose. It was as if I'd hit a slab of cold stone and I yelped.

The head grew bigger and moved closer, opening its mouth. I ain't seen nothing like it before, but if it had something to do with White Eye, I knew it would be evil through and through.

All of a sudden, Maymay's words 'bout evil spirits came flooding back to me. I sure as heck hoped I still had the Whippertonk Water. My hand shot into my pocket and pulled the bottle out. I flipped the lid off and threw the brown liquid at the gaping mouth.

Nothing happened.

My face fallen.

The head's menacing eyes locked on to mine and its mouth widened even further, its snowball-cold breath blasting my face. As I raised my arms to shield myself, it let out a heart-stopping scream and started to shrivel.

The other heads wound their necks in and a gap opened up. The young girl flung herself at White Eye.

The red fog started to dissolve. White Eye roared, raking at his arms and legs. He ballooned up to twice his size, his skin stretching tight. Without warning, his face and neck and chest split open as if they were made from tissue paper. Everyone who'd jumped into him, poured out of him and disappeared. Just as I let my breath out, one last person emerged from White Eye's remains.

I gawped, not sure whether to be happy or stiff-scared. *Was this really her?*

"The name of your dog is Point," said Maymay.

Relief washed over me. "Maymay, what the heck just happened?"

She kicked what was left of White Eye's papery body to one side. "White Eye crossed over to the spirit plane, which was fortunate 'cause this is where all my ancestors are. He forgot a little part of my soul was still inside him. With the assistance of my spirit guides, I was able to get each and every one of my dearly departed family to help me. White Eye has been reliant on the souls of others for so long, his own one had practically disappeared. You pouring the Whippertonk Water on him weakened him further. It's all thanks to you that me and my loved ones could drive him out of his own body. Even some of his victims showed up, only too glad to help out."

My bottom lip quivered. Maymay raised one of her eyebrows.

"We're in the spirit plane, ain't we? I'm so sorry. If I'd known you would lose your life I'd never have used Wah. It's all my fault you're here," I said, wiping my eyes.

Maymay's face softened. Even the black tear-shape in her eye didn't look so dark. "All great changes are preceded by a little chaos." She smiled.

My head bowed in shame.

"Twister, ain't you listened to a single word I've said? And to think all my wisdom has fallen on deaf ears. There ain't no such thing as death; my energy has simply switched to a different frequency. I can well and truly assure you there's life in me yet."

"Really?"

"Just you wait and see."

"Maymay," I said. "White Eye made Beam disappear. Will she ever come back?"

Before she could answer me, a rustling noise came from White Eye's remains. A grey mist appeared and swirled around on the ground. It grunted and snarled and bellowed and hissed.

"Uh . . . Maymay, I think he's still alive."

"You *are* listening, Twister. As you can see for yourself, death don't exist." Maymay sidestepped away from the noisy dust-devil. She bent down, picked up Wah and handed the necklace to me. Wah smiled at me as I put it in my pocket. I glanced at what was left of White Eye.

"Is this him changing into another sort of energy?"

"He is – and it's a formidable one. The darker souls that exist here are helping him."

"Can't you stop him?"

"This is where he belongs."

The mist turned into a thin whirling funnel. It stretched way up to touch the sky and disappeared.

A wind blew in strong. It poked the trees and got the crows all in a flap.

Maymay shouted over the noise. "Don't let White Eye stop you from getting back to the other side. You're a living being and if he succeeds you'll have no choice but to stay here for ever. Twig is your only way out."

Clouds gathered above us. All the colours in the woods dulled.

I hesitated. "Why didn't you tell me you'd met Pa? I know he gave you the necklace."

"You certainly pick your moments," said Maymay. "You asked me if I could help you, not if I'd met him in person."

I didn't move not one muscle. Maymay glanced at the sky. "The necklace was under a spell to stay hidden until it had chosen its next owner. When your pa brought it to me your name came up in conversation. Everything that my spirit guides had told me 'bout a twister being its owner finally made sense and I knew Wah was for you. I'm certain your pa never wanted you to have anything to do with the necklace. Happens I could not have agreed with him more; however, it was not our place to make that decision for you. It was your choice and your choice alone. Never let anyone take that away from you."

"Did he know 'bout White Eye?"

"I told him 'bout his existence. Whether he believed me or not is another matter."

"Is Pa here?"

"Not to my knowledge."

My heart fallen to the bottom of my ribcage. "Have you at any time had an inkling as to where he is?"

"No," said Maymay. "You must go now."

I stepped towards her.

"I ain't the hugging type," she said, backing away. "Besides, I'm sure we'll meet again."

I gave her one anyway. Squeezed her mighty hard too. What was she going to do? Change me into a bumpy toad?

Maymay released herself from me. "If you want to keep White Eye in the spirit plane, take his coat to the other side," she said. "Now go!"

I ran. The wind whipped at my skin. The grass blurred and the bushes waved and the ferns thrashed. The trees moaned and creaked and whined and clacked. Leaves darted past like frightened green birds.

Twig leant over at an angle. His white roots clung on to the ground for dear life. His mouth gnashed open and shut.

I heard a familiar sound over the cries of the wind. I stopped and turned. Point charged towards me, barking like crazy.

I glanced back at Twig. He'd blown over. If I didn't hurry, the wind might snatch him and my chance to escape away for good.

I threw myself at Point and wrapped my arms around him.

"I love you, Point. And I miss you every moment of every day."

Point whined. My eyes leaked. I buried my face into his soft black fur. "You come and see me as much as you can, you hear? I will always be watching for you."

There was an almighty explosion. A towering twister burst out from the woods. It stretched all the way from the grass up to the clouds. It was a vast churning mass of grey and white and black. It flickered with lightning flashes as it headed straight for us.

"Point – go find somewhere safe to shelter!" I yelled.

He bounded off towards Juniper Falls. It took all the strength I had not to follow him.

Everything rippled. I wiped my eyes and sprinted as fast as a pea out of a shooter towards Twig.

Leaves and dirt and dust and branches and grass and roots and petals and bird nests whistled past me. A sweetgum tree keeled over. One of its roots catched my foot and I tripped and fallen flat on my face. The twister was so close it was as if hundreds of hands were yanking at my clothes.

Twig rolled forwards and backwards on the ground. One by one, his roots snapped. If I didn't get to him now, I was going to be trapped here for ever.

I struggled to my feet, too frightened to look behind me. The wind was so loud, I couldn't hear my own thoughts.

I trip-stumbled the last few yards to Twig.

White Eye's raggedy coat flapped high up in the branches. I'd no time to lose. I climbed on to Twig's cracked trunk.

All of a sudden, there was an enormous gust of wind and Twig reared up, his branches raking at my body. The tree slammed back down. I was tossed on to the ground the same way a cowgirl is hurled off a bucking bronco.

The wind shrieked. More roots snapped. Twig's massive trunk rolled towards me. If it catched me, I'd be flattened.

I leapt out of the way as it thundered past. As soon as Twig came to a standstill, I spied White Eye's coat. I rushed towards it. The force of the wind slammed me into the tree. Black and red bruises blossomed all over my body.

With my last bit of energy, I reached out and snatched the coat. It was spiky and prickly and thorny and nippy and stingy. Critters swarmed up my arms. I swiped them off and untangled myself from the tree.

Lightning smashed the sky above.

I limped round to the other side of the trunk.

Twig's yellow eyes opened wide.

"Twig says: It's no use, Twister, you're too late; the time has come for you to meet your fate." He laughed one last time before his mouth started to close.

"No!" I cried out. I ripped off a branch to wedge Twig's jaws open with it. But it snapped as Twig's mouth slammed shut.

I fallen on to the grass and glanced towards the twister. Long and dark, it was tearing up the ground and whole trees were whirling 'bout inside it like matchsticks.

For a split-moment, I seen it stretch into the shape of White Eye. He leered at me.

The green grass turned gold. I swung round. That's when I noticed a ball of light, like a yellow pearl, wedged between Twig's teeth. Bit by bit it grew bigger. Twig's mouth began to open up, until it looked as if he was yawning.

Even though the wind was screaming, I heard a voice in my ears. "Hey. You won't get rid of me that easily. C'mon, Twistie! Jump! Can't hold him for much longer."

It was Beam! My heart flipped with joy.

I grabbed White Eye's rotten coat and leapt towards the light. I sailed past Twig's giant needle-like teeth. As I did so, I felt a hug, all cold as tin cans. Beam whispered,

"Forgot to thank you for saving my pa. You're the best friend ever."

Twig's mouth crunched shut behind me. The light vanished. I was in the dark with hundreds of pink eyes glaring at me. I crawled through Twig, sliding and slipping through the slime. In the distance, I spotted a white light. I'd be back in Holler Woods soon. I no longer felt the pain of the splinters pricking my skin.

The grass and the leaves and the sky and the clouds and the pollen and the herbs and the flowers and the earth and Juniper Falls had never smelled so good.

I was covered in cuts and bruises and scabs and welts and dirt and dust. But I didn't care two bits 'cause I'd made it back from the spirit plane. If Ma and Aunt Honey seen me now, they'd be sure to faint.

I got up, like a newborn foal attempting to stand for the first time. All bow legs and stumbles. I was one big all-over body ache.

Twig loomed over me, silent and white and spooky. His eyes and mouth had disappeared. It was as if they'd never existed. I prodded him with a stick. Nothing cracked or snapped or opened.

Holding White Eye's coat gave me the jeebie-heebies. I wanted to throw it away, so I'd never have to clap eyes on it again. But my guts niggled at me some. Maymay told me bringing the coat here would keep White Eye in the spirit plane. But what if he found a way to come back for it? The thought made my guts churn. There was only one thing I could do and that was to destroy it.

White Eye's coat tinkled. Gingerly, I opened it up to see what was making the noise. Inside, I found a whole load of different-coloured glass bottles. They must be filled with all the poor souls White Eye had stolen.

I took one out. It was the same colour as the ocean. A thought occurred to me. Perhaps it'd be best if I freed the souls, that way no one could ever steal them again.

I pulled the cork out.

A blue mist shot out of it. Before my eyes, it formed into the shape of a big bird with a fancy fan for a tail. It was a peacock! It shook its magnificent feathers and bowed. The peacock strutted around on the grass and called out. Its cry sounded much the same as a giant cat meowing. As it reached the trees, it faded and then with an almighty shake of its tail feathers, it vanished into thin air.

I grabbed as many bottles as I could and smashed them against Twig.

A whole rainbow of mists appeared around the white tree. Out from the colourful clouds ran a troop of monkeys. They swarmed up into the trees chattering excitedly. Every size and shape of bird flew up into the sky.

I could no longer see Twig. That's cause bang-slap in front of him stood an orange fire-breathing mountain!

Over by Juniper Falls, I spied a polar bear. That's right! A polar bear. As I live and breathe, it was the most spectacular creature I've ever laid eyes on. And when it dissolved into the sunbeams my eyes welled up. I wished it could have stayed for longer.

Laughter filled my ears. Lots of people appeared. I seen a fancy showgirl and a magician in a top hat and a leotard-wearing strongman. A girl stepped forward wearing a bright blue cape. She waved at me and I waved right on back at her. Children played tag with each other and cowboys fired their guns and a man wearing a gold crown galloped off on a horse.

I whooped with delight – releasing all these souls was the best feeling ever!

A huge shoal of every-colour-under-the-sun fish shot

out of the trees in a panic, a grey shark chasing after them. It skimmed over the tops of the bushes and headed straight for me. I ducked down as it passed over my head. With a flick of its tail, it glided towards Raging River.

There were so many souls, I was surprised the whole of Culleroy wasn't here to see what all the commotion was 'bout.

I felt around inside the icky-sticky coat. My fingers grasped the last remaining bottle. I brought it out. It was clear with a white stopper on it. As I held it up, the sun stretched down to touch it. It was cracked, but it shone so bright and pure, I didn't have the heart to smash it.

I twisted off the lid and set it down gently on the ground. The last swirl of mist curled out of the bottle. It swooshed and swished into the shape of a man.

I clasped my hands together, excited to see the last soul leaving its bottle-prison.

The man stepped forward. He was tall with white hair and had the biggest smile I've ever seen. His eyes were blue, bluer-than-blue.

It was Pa.

23

He reached out his arms and I fallen into them. I smelled soap and lemon and pepper and spice. I did not want to let go of him. Not *ever*.

"I've missed you." His voice was deep and warm and soothing.

"I was beginning to think I'd never find you," I said.

Pa pursed his lips. "I'm sorry for everything."

"Don't be. All you done was an act of kindness. You gave Maymay back a piece of jewellery that you thought belonged to her. You tried to warn me in your letter 'bout the necklace but I guess I'm just as stubborn as you."

"Maymay and I got talking the day I handed it to her. She said that her spirit guides had told her the necklace was meant for you. I thought she was crazy, especially when she started talking 'bout White Eye as if he was real. But then I remembered something. A terrible fire had broken out in Holler Woods, so me and some of the farm hands rushed over to help a family who were trapped."

"Turrety Knocks's family," I said.

"That's right," Pa answered.

"Aunt Honey told me everything."

Pa continued on, "We were beating the ground with our shirts, trying to stop the fire from spreading, when I glanced up and seen an old man standing across from us, watching. I noticed he had a white eye, but it struck me as peculiar that he wasn't doing anything to help. Before I could shout over to him, a tree came down and I was driven back by smoke. It had all happened so fast and it had been so hot, part of me wondered if I had imagined the whole thing. But the man having a white eye seemed more than just a coincidence, and made me wonder if what Maymay had said could be true. Seen my opportunity when someone came to her door. She'd told me if you wore it White Eye would know, so I slipped it on and figured if he was real, he'd come and find me. I insisted Maymay kept the necklace until I'd had time to think 'bout things. I returned home and waited. As a precaution, I wrote a letter and gave it to Turrety Knocks. He was in such a state 'bout losing his wife and child, I couldn't tell him what I'd just done. It didn't take long before White Eye appeared at the farm. He was much younger than the man I had remembered at the fire and his hair was a different colour, but as soon as I seen his eye, I knew White Eye was real. He was neither a man of words nor compassion; all he wanted was the necklace. When I swore I didn't have it, he took my life and stole my soul to punish me." Pa's eyes filled with so much sadness, he couldn't see me no more.

An ache spread its way around my body. I'd no idea it was possible to feel so happy and so sad, all at the same time. "It's OK, Pa," I said. "It's over now. White Eye ain't coming back from the spirit plane. All that matters is you're here. Ma and Aunt Honey are going to be beside themselves. Especially Ma. She's been so unwell. But you'll make her better again. Just you wait and see."

Pa's eyes found mine. "I never knew if I'd get the chance to see you again. This makes up for everything, being here with you now." He paused, taking a deep breath. "But life can't go back to the way it was, Twister. My soul has to move on to the next big adventure. That's just the way it has to be."

Pa began to fade. His colours were all washy-wishy. As if he was becoming a part of the land and the trees and the air.

"You be sure and look after your ma for me. You are the one she'll get better for. There are so many reasons you can all be a happy family again. Never forget that."

I felt Pa hugging me.

"Thank you, Twister," he said. "Thank you for not giving up on me. Thank you for having the courage to find me, and thank you for releasing me; I'm free now."

"Pa!" I cried out. "Please don't go!"

Everything was blurry. I frantically wiped the tears from my eyes, scared I'd lose sight of him.

I could no longer feel him next to me. I stepped back, seeing a faint shadow in front of the trees.

"I will never stop loving you all."

"Pa?"

"I will always be near, Twister."

And with that he vanished.

*

Noises floated up from the kitchen. Cupboards opened and closed. And plates and cutlery and glasses clattered down on the table. Aunt Honey and Ma were laughing together. Like they used to.

When I had made it home from Holler Woods, Ma and Aunt Honey had berry-red swollen eyes and faces pale as clouds. Aunt Honey said it looked as if I'd been to the ends of the earth and back. Which was funny 'cause I guess I kinda had, considering I'd been in the spirit plane and all. I said that I'd escaped from Hack Hussable and made it to Juniper Falls where I'd hidden in a cave. That went some ways to explaining the bruises and cuts and bumps and lumps and scrapes on my skin. I hated fibbing, but they'd be sure to lock me away for being loopy-pinto if I told them the truth.

Once they'd bathed me and near dabbed me raw with antiseptic-soaked cotton balls, they tucked me up tightly in bed.

Time passed 'cause Ma and Aunt Honey kept appearing by my bedside wearing different clothes. Their brows were furled and they insisted on pressing their hands against my forehead.

One afternoon, Aunt Honey propped me up on

plumped pillows. She told me Turrety Knocks and Neeps had moved into one of the outhouses. Turrety Knocks was fixing the barn and would earn his meals doing odd jobs around the farm. Aunt Honey wore perfume. It stank very much like sweet peas and gave me a headache. But I kept that to myself.

Aunt Honey's eyes grew big as full moons when she told me 'bout Hack Hussable. He'd been arrested by Sheriff Buckstaffy and charged with the attempted murder of Turrety Knocks and setting fire to the barn. The blue naked lady on Hack's arm sure would be pale and wrinkly by the time he got his first taste of freedom.

Clem hadn't got the sight back in his eye yet. Milda Hussable had had enough of Hack's sly words and handy fists. She packed their bags and moved far away to a place Hack would never find them. I was glad I'd never have to bump into Clem again. I couldn't forgive him for what he'd done to Point, but I hoped a life finally free from Hack might make Clem happy. And a happy Clem would be a whole lot safer to be around than an unhappy one.

Beam came to visit in the dead of night. Pitching up when I least expected it and giving me a fright as usual, but I was glad of her company. It gave me the chance to thank her for helping me escape from the spirit plane. We swore never to fall out with each other again. She tried her best to cheer me up with all the latest tales from Holler Woods. And promised to help me destroy White Eye's coat as soon as I felt better.

Ma sat with me too. She poured hot soup down my neck. And forced me to sip yucky potions with herbs in them. Some of them got flung straight out the window, I can tell you.

Ma no longer drifted off to other places. And if I yelled in my sleep, she'd lie beside me until my breathing became deep and slow again. One night, when she thought I'd gone to dreamland, she whispered that she heard the gate squeak open every night, but nobody was ever there.

My bruised heart thumped painfully.

Ma stroked my hair and told me she was sorry. Sorry that I'd not only lost Pa, but at times it must have felt like I'd lost her too. My disappearance after the fire in the barn had given her such a fright, she said all she wanted to do was to get well again. And she vowed she'd take better care of me from here on in.

Each week that passed, my pain and sadness hurt a little

less so. Like an open wound being covered by a thin scab.

Aunt Honey bumped into Miss Ida, who'd said she'd be mighty pleased to see me back in class. I started pinching my nose and drinking Ma's potions. I even took short walks around the farm. I'd search the shadows for Pa, but I couldn't see nothing. Worse still, I couldn't even sense him. My heart plain broke in four. On the days I was too tired to be sad or angry, I'd sit on high walls and talk to the wind. I hoped it'd take my words to Pa's ears.

I got out of bed and stretched and threw on my T-shirt and shorts.

When I made the stairs creak, the voices in the kitchen went hushety-quiet. Ma and Aunt Honey and Turrety Knocks beamed at me as I walked into the room. Even Mew jumped off the cupboard to rub her soft head against my leg.

"Here she is! Oh my! Ain't you a picture when your hair's brushed," said Aunt Honey. "Today we have for your delight: eggs, bacon, pancakes, hash browns and orange juice. Otherwise known as brain-food. After this, you'll stun Miss Ida with your abundance of knowledge and keenness to learn. Just you see." Aunt Honey winked at me.

Ma waved for me to sit at the table. "Are you sure you're able to go to school, Twister?" she asked. "I still think you're looking a bit peaky."

"Now, stop fussing, Ma. It'll do her good to get out from under our feet," said Aunt Honey.

I'm not right sure what she meant 'cause I wasn't nowhere near their feet. "I'm fine, Ma, honestly, I am," I said.

Turrety Knocks shuffled forward clutching a brown box. He'd combed his hair flat and his clothes had been darned shut. I swear the sparkle was back in his moss and bark eyes.

"This is for you, Twister. Found her tied in a bag by Raging River. Your ma and Honey says it's OK for you to have her."

Something scratched inside the box. I glanced from Ma to Aunt Honey to Turrety Knocks. They all nodded for me to open it. Even Mew leapt on to the table to see what all the fuss was 'bout.

I lifted the lid. There in the corner sat a ball of toffee-coloured fluff. It was a puppy! Careful as careful could be, I picked her up.

The room filled with *awww*-ing. Mew wasn't quite so enthusiastic though. She flung herself off the table, refusing to glance at any of us on her way out the door.

I gazed into the puppy's eyes. They were the same colour as golden syrup. And so beautiful, I missed them every time she blinked. "Thank you, Turrety Knocks. I *love* her."

Turrety Knocks leant forward. "She's smart and full of pluck, same as you."

"What you going to call her, Twist?" asked Ma.

The sun shone in through the kitchen window, making her fur gleam. At that very moment, she sneezed. Her top lip got stuck on her teeny-tiny white teeth. It looked very much like she was giving me a goofy smile.

"Everyone," I said. "Meet Grin."

Aunt Honey swooped in and took Grin from me. "Inspired choice of name, Twister. I hate to be the one to break the party up, but you need to eat your breakfast, otherwise you'll be late for school."

She placed Grin on the floor and plonked a plate in front of me. I couldn't see the pattern on it 'cause it was heaped with so much food.

Today sure was going to be a good day. I could tell.

The black rooster on what was left of the barn roof twirled round and round and round. And the clouds played tag with each other across the sky.

Gorgeous George and Peckers the hen squabbled with each other. All the other hens clucked 'bout it too. Proudfoot snorted in his field and Gloria and Merle merrily swished their tails. Swayback was busy bathing in the mud. But he stopped as soon as he seen us in the yard. As I said before, he was a mighty prissy hog.

"Have you got your packed lunch?" asked Aunt Honey.

"Yes, Aunt Honey."

"Good! We can't have you fainting with hunger, can we?" said Aunt Honey.

"That won't happen anytime soon," I laughed.

"Twist, want me to walk you to school? said Ma.

"Thanks all the same but I'm fine, Ma."

"Are you certain 'bout going back today, Twist?" asked Ma. "I could tell Miss Ida you'll be there tomorrow instead?"

"I'm sure," I said, nodding.

"Want me to look after Grin while you're in class?" asked Turrety Knocks.

"Thanks, Turrety Knocks," I said. "That'd be much appreciated."

We made our way to the gate with the grace of a circus troupe. Grin tried to keep up with us, but she kept on tripping over her huge ears. Turrety Knocks scooped her up and tucked her safely under his arm. She sneezed and grinned at us.

I opened the gate.

Ma and Aunt Honey and Turrety Knocks stood in a line behind it. Beam appeared too, standing next to her pa.

"Hey, Twistie. Have a great day at school. See you after at Raging River if you fancy catching some green fish?" she yelled.

I nodded and waved at her, careful not to shout anything back that would give the game away she was there. If Ma and Aunt Honey thought I was talking to an invisible person they'd cart me off to the hospital in Pineville. Turrety Knocks wouldn't though. He'd know exactly who I was chatting to.

I strolled on down the path. I put my hand in my pocket. My fingers grasped a small, cool glass bottle. I knew Pa wasn't in it any more – but it reminded me how lucky I was getting the chance to see him one last time.

And that made me happy.

As I turned to give them all a final wave, Aunt Honey hollered after me. "Pay attention in class, Twist! Smart ladies attract good husbands. Bees to honey, I tell you. Bees to honey." Beam snorted with laughter.

I smiled. The trees along the path swayed in the wind. They bowed their heads and clapped their leaves as I passed them by. Insects were clicking and sawing and chomping and scuttling and pulsing and fluttering in the sunshine.

The birds were singing songs and preening their feathers and darting through the trees and sifting the earth for fat worms. Everything was living its life to the full for it wasn't possible to guess what tomorrow would bring.

I didn't need Wah to show me what was floating in the air. It'd be filled with all kinds of soul bubbles. They'd be smacking off my arms and legs. Getting catched in my hair and flashing and twirling and spinning in front of my eyes. If I could see them, they'd be full of children playing and sleepy mountains and thundering rivers and swaying trees and bright flowers and gulping fish and fluttering butterflies and cotton-ball clouds. There may even be a tiger or a pirate or a wizard or a queen in amongst them.

Maymay was back in her cabin in Holler Woods. She must be a ghost now, though you'd never guess. Who knows, maybe she'd always been a spooky ghost. I thought it best not to ask her, in case I upset her feelings. I pleaded with her to keep Wah. Well, you know Maymay, she plain refused. She said it'd only find its way back to me and offered me a Pomple Root Crunch instead.

Beam and me borrowed Turrety Knocks's rickety boat. We rowed out to the island on Cedar Creek Lake. The first thing I done was to burn White Eye's coat. Huge red and black flames shot out of it. Beam and me had to duck behind a bush 'cause of all the sparks that flew around. I was right happy when it finally turned into a pile of ash. The thought of White Eye roaming 'bout the spirit plane made me shiver. There was no way I ever wanted to see him again.

Now there really is treasure on the island 'cause that's where I hid Wah and ain't nobody was ever going to find it. Apart from me and Beam, that was. I decided that best friends should tell each other 100% everything from now on.

I'll miss Wah's smile but I don't want to use the necklace no more. If I ever need strength or guts or brains or courage or spirit or hope or happiness, all I had to do was take a deep breath and concentrate. Whatever I wanted was right here, inside of me. And there wasn't nothing I couldn't face now that I knew that.

Miss Ida rang the school bell. I didn't want to be late on my first day back otherwise she might give me extra arithmetic.

A breeze tickled my skin and the sun shone brightly between the thick tree trunks. I started to run. Everything was light and dark and light and dark and light and dark.

I wasn't right sure, but it was as if two shadows were running alongside me. One was like a black dog with its ears flapping crazily in the wind. And the other looked very much like Pa was where he said he'd be. Right by my side.

ACKNOWLEDGEMENTS

Thank heavens I'm awful at painting, otherwise I might never have left my art class to do a course in creative writing. The teacher, Ian Macpherson, was (and still is) an inspiration and this is all his fault because he was the one who suggested I write a book. Thank you, Ian, and I'm sorry for thinking you had taken leave of your senses.

None of this would have been possible without Keith Gray and the wonderful Scottish Book Trust, who made me a New Writer awardee, sent me on writing retreats and introduced me to my mentor, Julie Bertagna. Julie's sage advice helped me whip everything into shape and led to me contacting the Greenhouse Literary Agency. Polly, you are one in a million – even though you make me cry more than anyone else, what with championing my writing and getting me terrific publishing deals.

A massive thank you to Lauren Fortune for backing *Twister* from the get-go. With a wave of your magic editing wand, everything now shines so much brighter. And I'm most grateful to Pete Matthews for gallantly fixing my bloopers. The Scholastic team are an incredible bunch and have blown me away with their hard work and enthusiasm. I must give special mention to the visionary Sean Williams and to Alexis Snell, who transformed the novel into a work of art with her stunning lino-cut prints.

Thank you, Ali Taylor, for our WINE (writers in need of encouragement) nights. I'm so lucky to have your support, feedback, wit and positivity. You are a force to be reckoned with, as are Mark's holiday wines.

Mum, Dad and Robert – did I mention I was penning a children's book? I hope your ears are not hurting too much from my constant twittering. I am extremely thankful, Dad, for you reading the manuscript when you did.

And lastly, to my cousin, Lara; your belief in me is astonishing and has been my rock throughout. Here's to many more crazy adventures exploring the four corners of the world.

Photo by Susan Castillo

ABOUT THE AUTHOR

Juliette Forrest has worked as both an art director and a copywriter for some of the best advertising agencies in the UK and in 2014 won a New Writers Award from the Scottish Book Trust. Juliette lives in Glasgow where she runs her own freelance copywriting business.